Dummie the Mummy
and the Golden
scarab

For my dear friend Erik

www.dummiethemummy.com

ISBN 978 90 00 35784 0
ISBN 978 90 00 32183 4 e-book
NUR 284

Originally published in Dutch © 2009 Van Goor
English translation © 2018 Van Goor
Uitgeverij Unieboek | Het Spectrum bv
P.O. Box 97, 3990 DB Houten, The Netherlands

www.toscamenten.nl
www.beeldvanhees.nl
www.de-leukste-kinderboeken.nl

text Tosca Menten
illustrations and design Elly Hees
translation Michele Hutchinson
typeset Mat-Zet bv, Soest

Tosca Menten

Dummie the Mummy

and the Golden Scarab

with illustrations
by Elly Hees

Translated by
Michele Hutchison

Van Goor

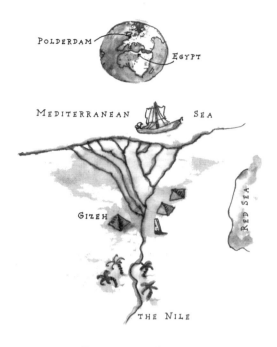

POLDERDAM

EGYPT

MEDITERRANEAN SEA

RED SEA

GIZEH

THE NILE

EGYPT

SECOND YEAR IN THE REIGN OF AKHNETUT THE FIRST

IT WAS QUIET IN THE PALACE.
OMINOUSLY QUIET. AS THOUGH SOMETHING
TERRIBLE WAS ABOUT TO HAPPEN.

DARWISHI UR-ATUM MSAMAKI MINKABH
ISHAQ EBONI, SON OF PHARAOH AKHNETUT I
AND HIS WIFE ENISIS, WAS LYING IN BED IN
THE COOLEST ROOM IN THE PALACE. NOT
THAT IT HELPED. DARWISHI WAS BOILING HOT.

HE HAD NEVER BEEN THIS HOT.

SOMEONE WAVED A FAN, BUT IT REMAINED HOT. SOMEONE GAVE HIM WATER, BUT IT DIDN'T HELP. NOTHING HELPED.

DARWISHI'S FATHER AND MOTHER WERE SITTING TO THE LEFT AND RIGHT OF HIS BED. THEY WERE WHISPERING.

THE HIGH PRIEST HEPSETSUT CAME INTO THE ROOM AND WHISPERED TOO. EVERYONE WAS WHISPERING AND TIPTOEING.

THE HOTTER DARWISHI GOT, THE QUIETER IT BECAME.

HE SUDDENLY HAD A TERRIBLE THOUGHT. "DO I HAVE TO GO AWAY?" HE ASKED.

"YES. YOU HAVE TO GO AWAY, SON." THE PHARAOH SAID.

"RIGHT NOW? BUT I WANT TO STAY HERE," DARWISHI SAID ANXIOUSLY. "OR ARE YOU COMING WITH ME?"

HIS FATHER SHOOK HIS HEAD.

"BUT I'M NOT ALLOWED TO TRAVEL ALONE, AM I?"

"YOU'RE NOT GOING ALONE," THE PHARAOH SAID. "THE SCARAB OF MUKATAGARA IS COMING WITH YOU. HE WILL PROTECT YOU ON THE WAY."

DARWISHI DIDN'T UNDERSTAND. THE SCARAB OF MUKATAGARA FROM HIS FATHER'S CROWN? THE SCARAB THAT HIS FATHER HAD TOLD HIM PROTECTED THE COUNTRY? THE MOST POWERFUL SCARAB IN THE ENTIRE KINGDOM

WAS GOING TO COME WITH HIM? BUT HE
DIDN'T WANT THE SCARAB! HE WANTED TO
STAY HERE!

"AND WHAT ABOUT YOU THEN?" DARWISHI
ASKED AFTER A WHILE.

"WE WILL THINK OF YOU," HIS MOTHER
WHISPERED.

"WILL THAT HELP?" DARWISHI ASKED.

"YES, IT WILL HELP," HIS MOTHER SAID. "GO
TO SLEEP NOW."

"ALRIGHT," LITTLE DARWISHI SAID BRAVELY.

THOSE WERE HIS LAST WORDS. HE GOT SO
HOT THAT IT MADE HIM GO TO SLEEP AND
NEVER WAKE UP.

HIS FATHER AND MOTHER WERE THE SADDEST
PEOPLE IN EGYPT. THEY TORE OUT THEIR HAIR
AND CRIED UNTIL THEY HAD RUN OUT OF
TEARS.

THEN THE PHARAOH CALLED FOR
HEPSETSUT. THE SMALL BOY WAS EMBALMED
FOR SEVENTY DAYS AND WRAPPED IN LINEN
BANDAGES. THEN HE WAS READY FOR HIS
JOURNEY TO THE AFTERWORLD.

THE PHARAOH TOOK THE SCARAB OUT OF
HIS CROWN AND HUNG IT ON A SMALL IRON
CHAIN. "HEPSETSUT, GIVE HIM THE SCARAB,"
HE WHISPERED.

THE HIGH PRIEST LOOKED AT HIM IN
DISBELIEF.

"GIVE IT TO HIM AND SAY THE HOLY WORDS.

I PROMISED HIM THIS. IT IS WHAT I WANT.
GIVE THE GOLDEN SCARAB OF MUKATAGARA
TO MY SON."

THE HIGH PRIEST CAREFULLY HUNG THE
POWERFUL AMULET AROUND DARWISHI'S NECK
AND PUSHED IT DOWN BETWEEN THE BANDAGES.

"SPEAK," THE PHARAOH SAID.

THE HIGH PRIEST SPOKE. NEXT TO THE
SARCOPHAGUS, HE MUTTERED FOR TWENTY-
FOUR HOURS ON END. FINALLY HE PRESSED
A SMALL BOOK BETWEEN THE BANDAGES AS
WELL. "I HAVE DONE EVERYTHING I CAN," HE
SAID.

"THEN WE WILL BURY HIM IN SILENCE," THE
PHARAOH SAID.

TWELVE BEARERS CARRIED THE HEAVY
SARCOPHAGUS INTO THE SMALL BURIAL
CHAMBER. A MASON CARVED SIX NAMES INTO
THE WALL:

DARWISHI

UR-ATUM

MSAMAKI

MINKABH

ISHAQ

EBONI.

"HAVE A SAFE JOURNEY," THE PHARAOH
WHISPERED. "MAY THE SCARAB OF
MUKATAGARA PROTECT YOU."

THEN THEY CLOSED THE DOOR. FOREVER,
EVERYONE THOUGHT.

the Netherlands
21ST Century A.D.

Rudy Woodman was driving along the road in his truck. It was cold, but Rudy was warm. He was a bear of a man with a tangle of curls, a muscular neck and dragon tattoos on one arm, and he wasn't afraid of any living thing. But he was scared to death of anything that was dead. And now he was driving to The Grobbe Museum with three mummies in his truck. An extra run, his boss had said. If he had known beforehand what kind of run his boss had meant, he would never have agreed to it.

The Grobbe Museum was just an hour away. But for Rudy a whole hour with three mummies in his container seemed an eternity. As the engine of his truck hummed, he listened with one ear to the suspicious noises coming from behind him.

He wasn't even five minutes into his journey when it started to rain. And not just a bit, water came bucketing out of the sky. Rudy stared out of his windscreen and couldn't see a thing. Then it began to thunder as well.

The first flash of lightning shot through the air just as Rudy was pulling onto the motorway. Shortly afterwards, the storm reached a climax. "That's all I need," Rudy muttered. "Next thing I know, I'll be crashing with these horrid things in the back."

He put his windscreen wipers onto the fastest setting and squinted. "Rats!"

Rudy had just said "rats" for the tenth time when lightning hit the truck.

There was a great big bang and Rudy was temporarily blinded. The truck hit the crash barrier, metal screeched and a rain of sparks spattered against Rudy's window. An instant later he was hurtling upside down from the viaduct. "Aargh! Helllllp!" Rudy screamed. He didn't stop screaming until he had crashed to a stop against the only tree around.

"Rats," Rudy whispered when it was quiet again. He carefully moved his arms and legs. When everything seemed to work, he scrambled clumsily out of the battered cab. He collapsed to the ground and looked around. There wasn't much left of the truck. There were bits of debris everywhere, and two large coffins amongst them. The third coffin was a few metres away, half-open. Thick diesel streamed from the broken petrol tank.

It took a while to sink in. Lightning. A high tree. Diesel... Get out of there! Rudy hurriedly got to his feet and staggered away.

Out of the corner of his eye, he suddenly saw something move. He turned his head and jumped out of his skin. A few metres away, a white arm was sticking out of a ditch. Another arm appeared. And a head! A small white shape slowly emerged. Rudy stared at the terrifying apparition in horror.

The shape stood up, took a few wobbly steps, fell and

scrambled to its feet again. All of a sudden it turned around and looked Rudy right in the face.

Rudy's heart nearly stopped. He thought: Get out of here. If you don't run away, it will get you! But his legs wouldn't move. He thought: Scream then. Shout! Scare him!

"Boo," Rudy groaned.

The shape stayed where it was.

"Boo! Go away! Boo! Hellllp!"

The thing took a step towards him.

"Eurgh! Aargh! Whaaaaaaah!" Rudy screamed.

BANG!

The next lightning strike hit the tree. A deafening thunderclap made the ground shake as though a herd of elephants was stampeding past. Dazed, Rudy saw the large tree fall. Suddenly his legs started working again. He ran like the wind. The tree toppled onto the wreck, the diesel burst into flames and a few seconds later the entire truck exploded. Rudy was hurled to the ground. He looked at the fireball in dismay. And then at the ditch. The figure had disappeared without a trace.

Half an hour later, the fire brigade had put out the blaze.

Two policemen questioned Rudy in the pouring rain.

"What was in your truck, sir?" asked the tallest of the pair.

"Mummies," Rudy muttered. "Three mummies. With sarcophagi and the lot."

"Terrible shame," the policeman said, shaking his head. "Well, at least they were already dead."

"No, no, one of them survived," Rudy blurted out.

"Survived?" the policeman asked.

"Yes, a little one," Rudy said, "but he ran away."

"Aha!" The tall policeman winked at his colleague.

"And which way did he go?" he asked, feigning interest.

"T-t-that way, I think," Rudy said, as he pointed in the direction.

Both policemen pretended to write something down.

"Don't worry, sir. We'll catch him," they said in a friendly tone.

"He's taken quite a blow to the head," the tall policeman whispered.

"Or the mummy got to him," the small one laughed.

Suddenly Rudy began to doubt himself. It could have been the blow. He got carried away by his imagination. Those horrible things had almost been the death of him. From now on he was going to deliver nothing but apples for the rest of his life.

DARWISHI UR-ATUM MSAMAKI MINKABH ISHAQ EBONI RAN THROUGH THE RAIN.

WHERE WAS THE SAND OF THE DESERT?
WHERE WERE THE HOUSES? THE MARKET
STALLS? THE PALACE? HE RAN, FELL, STOOD
UP AND RAN SOME MORE. AWAY FROM THE
FIRE. AWAY FROM THAT ROARING NOISE.
AWAY FROM THAT STRANGE MAN WHO WAS
POINTING AT HIM LIKE HE'D SEEN A LION.

DARWISHI LOOKED BACK. AN ENORMOUS
FIREBALL. BLACK SMOKE. SCREAMING.
SCREECHING SHINY CARTS.

WAS THIS THE UNDERWORLD?

HE RAN AND RAN AND THOUGHT: MY NAME
IS DARWISHI UR-ATUM MSAMAKI MINKABH
ISHAQ EBONI AND I AM GOING ON A JOURNEY.
HEPSETSUT. THE SCARAB!

HE STOPPED AND FELT UNDER HIS
BANDAGES FOR THE GOLDEN PENDANT IN
THE MIDDLE OF HIS CHEST. HE CLAMPED HIS
FINGERS TIGHTLY AROUND IT AND LISTENED.

THE CARTS SCREECHED IN THE DISTANCE.
THE ONLY OTHER THING HE COULD HEAR WAS
HIS OWN PANTING. PANTING? HE HEARD
HIS OWN PANTING!

HE WAS ALIVE! BUT WHERE WAS HE? AND
WHERE SHOULD HE GO?

IN DESPERATION, HE BEGAN TO RUN AGAIN.

CHAPTER 1
Dummie
the Mummy

The most amazing things happened to Angus Gust. He took trips to the North Pole in a submarine, he won the lottery, he was the first ten-year old to be allowed to travel to Mars and he became world famous for being able to play the recorder with his toes. That wasn't all, he could talk to things too. If he said, "Knife, why don't you cut the bread properly?" the knife would reply, "Because I don't want to cut right now. I'm not feeling that sharp today." That was a good joke coming from a knife and Angus split his sides laughing. Another time he had a row with a door which wouldn't close and with a sock which had hidden from him.

All in all, Angus was simply the most special child

in the entire world. Well, in his own imagination, he
was.

Angus' real life was terribly normal. That was
because he lived in Polderdam. Polderdam was the
most boring village in the country. And probably in the
whole world. Nothing ever happened to people who
lived in Polderdam.

Angus lived with his father Nick in an old house
outside the village. To be honest, he looked as normal
as the rest of the children in Polderdam. He had
normal brown hair, blue eyes and his nose wasn't flat,
nor was his chin pointy or anything. Yes, his face was
covered in freckles, but other children in his class had
freckles too. He wasn't particularly good or particularly
bad at anything and he wasn't cool either. And he
didn't hate anybody, only a couple of girls in his class.
And Miss Frick too, of course. But everyone hated her.

Every day Angus just went to school and got normal grades. Then he went home again and just did normal things, like watching TV and playing games. Or he cooked. He had to, because sometimes his father was too busy. Angus couldn't cook, so usually he just fried six eggs and he and his father ate them with bread.

Nick Gust was an artist and painted paintings which nobody bought. His whole shed was full of them. But it also meant he was always home and so Nick and Angus could do everything together. They looked after each other (Nick looked after Angus a bit more than the other way round) and they had lots of fun together. Nick rarely got angry, only at his paintings. He swore at them and said things like, "Ugly cottypot!" It was a swearword he had specially invented, because Angus and his father did not allow swearing in the house. He had also invented "Whumpy dumpman" and he used that for all other things. When he shouted "Ugly cottypot!" it meant his painting had gone wrong. Then he'd wave his paintbrushes angrily and wipe more paint on his trousers than on the canvas. He would get furious about it, but Angus couldn't help finding it funny.

"Do you think it's any fun being a painter?" Nick would roar when this happened.

"Then you should do something else!" Angus would laugh.

"No! I can't do anything else!" Nick would shout.

And then Angus would say that his father couldn't paint either, and that he'd be better off framing his trousers, because they looked like a painting too by now.

Angus could say that kind of thing to his father. Angus could say anything he wanted to his father, because he didn't have anyone else. Until Dummy turned up at their house, at least.

A little while ago, Angus had also invented his own swearword. At first it was "Poopy dingle" but after a day he had changed it to "Blasting cackdingle". That sounded angrier.

Nick had roared with laughter. "You've got a good imagination, son," he'd chuckled.

"I've got it from you," Angus had said.

And that's how things were between Angus and Nick. Despite the fact that they lived in a boring village, they had a good time, just the two of them. They both thought so. Although, Nick had recently said that perhaps it wasn't such a good thing that Angus never played with other children.

"I've got you, though," Angus had replied. "And my imagination. And our house with all our talking things and all of their stories."

"I still think it would be good if you played with other children," Nick said.

"I'm doing alright, aren't I?" Angus asked.

"Sure, you're doing alright," his father replied quickly.

"Well then," Angus said.

After that they hadn't mentioned it again. They were happy with just the two of them. And Angus had never expected that to change.

Until Dummie arrived.

On that strange evening, Angus and his father were sitting at the table. Nick had cooked and they were eating macaroni and broccoli. Nick put broccoli in everything because broccoli has lots of vitamins, he said.

There was a storm blowing outside.

"The clouds are having an argument," Angus said, with his mouth full. "BIL HENNAH IL SHIFFA."

"Slafsa saliki?" his father wanted to know.

Angus burst out laughing. "BIL HENNAH IL SHIFFA" is Egyptian for enjoy your food. Mr Scribble taught us that. I told you about the schools' competition about Egypt, didn't I? That's in a couple of month's time. And now we have to learn about Egypt every day."

"Shouldn't you be learning maths?" Nick asked.

"We do, in between," Angus said. "But I think the competition is more important to Mr Scribble. He took all the maps down off the wall. And now there are all kinds of posters in the classroom, of pyramids and stuff like that. Of a golden mask from one of those dead pharaohs."

"Tutankhamun," Nick said.

"Yes, that one." Angus took another mouthful of food. "Can we go on holiday to Egypt?"

"If I sell a few paintings," his father said.

This meant no. Nick had once inherited some money and it had allowed them to buy food and paint. But they had to scrimp and save, and they never went on holiday.

"It's not as expensive as you think," Angus said. "You only need swimming trunks. Then we'll go and feed the crocodiles in the Nile. And climb the pyramids. And then we'll visit the graves. And then we'll discover a secret burial chamber, where no one has been before, and it will have ten of those coffins in it."

"Sarcophagi," his father said.

"Yes, those. And we'll find the treasure and we'll be rich."

"And then one of those mummies will take revenge on us," Nick chuckled. "You won't catch me there. We'll just stay here in our own home. No money and no cares. But we have each other."

"MAASHI," Angus said. "That's Egyptian for OK."

They had finished. Nick went to the shed to wash his brushes and Angus cleared the table. Then he went upstairs.

That is where Angus saw him.

At first he didn't notice him. He went into his bedroom and smelled something disgusting. Angus immediately thought back to a month previously, when he had smelled something like that and there had been a mouse rotting in the attic. Now it smelled like an entire family of mice were rotting. Angus giggled, his father would have to go up into the attic again. Nick hated the attic, it hit him on the head every ten seconds with its broad beams. Last time he had shouted "Whumpy dumpman!" at least ten times, and after that a real swearword too.

Angus decided immediately to tell his father a bit later, picked up a book and threw back his duvet. He jumped out of his skin. He was too shocked to even shout. He recoiled in horror. There was something in his bed. Or someone. Or rather something than someone. He shook his head but it didn't make any difference. He squeezed his eyes shut, but when he opened them again, the thing was still lying there. It looked just like the thing on one of the posters in his classroom. That was a mummy. A mummy was lying in his bed. A mummy?!

Angus just stood there for at least thirty seconds. Then he slapped his forehead. Dad, he thought. He'd fallen for it again. His father had pulled a practical joke on him. Nick had already put a scarecrow on the toilet once. That was a joke too. Angus had peed his pants in fright and his father had split his sides laughing. That might sound mean, but a week earlier, Angus had been the one to scare his father. He had painted himself green, and he had jumped into his father's studio beeping like an alien, almost giving Nick a heart attack. At least, that was what he said.

So now his father had made a fake mummy as punishment. Well, he had done a good job, with tattered old bits of bandage. And the smell was also very convincing. Stink bombs perhaps. Angus chuckled and decided to drag the thing to his father's bed. Or no, he'd put it in the car. That would be a good joke!

He approached the bed smiling to himself.

"ɢʀᴀᴀɢʜ, ᴡʜʀᴀᴀɢ," the mummy groaned.

Angus nearly fell backwards in surprise. Blasting cackdingle! The thing could make a noise! It moved! It... it got up!

Angus didn't wait any longer, but flew out of the

room, slammed the door and leaned against it. His heart was racing. That wasn't a doll! The mummy was alive! He had seen it with his own eyes. Hadn't he? Hey? Was he going mad?

He opened the door and cautiously peered through the chink. He wasn't going mad. The mummy swung both of his legs out of the bed, sat on the edge and looked out of the window. It was open a little. That's how he got in, Angus realised in a flash.

The mummy obviously hadn't seen Angus. He

stood up and began to nose around. He picked up
a pen from Angus' desk, held it up to his head and
dropped it again, he did the same with a few books, a
notebook and a pair of socks. Meanwhile he babbled
away, "GHLEITSA" and "GHOTEP" and words like that.
Then he picked up Angus' radio. He turned a dial and
all of a sudden loud music blared out. The mummy
was terrified. He dropped the radio and dived under
Angus' bed. Normally Angus would have roared with
laughter, but no sound came out of his mouth.

After a while, the mummy crawled out from
under the bed again and tiptoed towards the radio.
He bent down, listened and all of a sudden gave the
radio a big whack. "SIRSAR!" he hissed. The music
stopped immediately. The mummy said something
else foreign, maybe it was "hooray" or "I won" or
something like that. Next he walked to Angus'
wardrobe and began to make a big mess of all the
clothes. When he'd finished, he started trampolining
on the bed, jumping from the pillow onto the duvet
and back again.

Angus had had enough. He wasn't going to wait
until the mummy had destroyed his entire bedroom,
he had to fetch his father!

He closed the door and ran downstairs.

Nick was sitting in his red armchair in front of the
television with his eyes closed. He often had a nap
there. He did this every evening and Angus wasn't
allowed to speak to him for half an hour, unless the
house was on fire. If there was a mummy in the house,
it was probably alright too.

"Dad! Dad!" a flustered Angus shouted, shaking Nick by the shoulder.

"Quiet, I'm sleeping," Nick said with his eyes closed.

"Dad! There's a— There's a—" Angus faltered. Should he just say that there was a mummy in his bedroom that stank of dead mice and had whacked his radio?

"Is there a fire?" his father asked.

"No. But—"

"Well, out with it then!" his father said impatiently. And when Angus remained silent, "Just tell me what it is!"

"Alright. There's someone in my bedroom. A mum—"

"What? A burglar?" Nick jumped up, suddenly wide awake, and rushed to the door.

"Stop! Wait a minute, Dad. It's not a burglar."

"A tramp who's broken in then? Stay here. I'll get that tramp—"

"Dad! It's not a tramp either!" Angus cried. "There's a mummy in my bedroom!"

His father stood stock still. "What kind of a mummy?" he asked foolishly.

"You know, the kind made of loads of bandages with a dead person inside!"

"Whumpy dumpman!" Nick tapped the side of his forehead with his finger. "You won't get me to fall for that one. Son, give up on the jokes. You'll give me another heart attack."

"I'm not lying! There's a mummy upstairs! Don't you believe me?"

"No!" Nick said.

"But it's really true! We have to do something!"

Angus gave his father a pleading look.

"Now, that's enough," Nick said. "I'll come upstairs with you. If it turns out that mummy of yours has taken off, you'll be grounded for a week. And if there is a mummy in your bedroom, I'll eat my hat."

"Well, I wouldn't do that, Dad. You'll upset your stomach," Angus said.

"There's nothing wrong with my stomach," Nick said. "Upstairs with you, come on."

They climbed the stairs. When they had reached the top, Angus quickly stationed himself in front of his bedroom door. "I want you to be nice to him," he said.

"Angus, step aside," his father said.

"Promise me. You mustn't frighten him."

"Angus!"

"Only if—"

"Out of the way!" Nick threw the door open, walked in and looked around. "There you are, you see. No one."

"No one?" Angus rushed past his father and looked around his room in dismay. He looked out of the window but the garden was empty. There wasn't anyone under his bed or under his desk. "He's gone! He's gone!" he wailed.

"Homesick for Egypt, I take it," Nick joked. He closed the window and turned around. "What a mess. And what's that horrible smell?"

"That's all because of the mummy. Don't you see I'm telling the truth?"

Now his father was getting irritated. "Just give it up, will you!" he shouted.

There was a noise from inside the wardrobe.

Nick turned around with a start. "What was that?"

"That's him. He's in the wardrobe!" Angus was almost triumphant.

"I'm going mad," Nick said. He went over to the wardrobe and jerked it open. "I—" He shut his mouth again. His eyes widened and he took a step backwards.

"Can you see anything?" Angus asked, playing the innocent.

Nick opened and closed his mouth. "Angus, there's a mummy in the wardrobe," he said at last.

A moment later, Nick was doing what every father would probably have done in that situation. He grabbed the first weapon he could lay his hands on (in this case a ruler), stepped protectively in front of Angus, and started to shout as loudly as he could, "Get out of there, you! Move! Psst! Go away!"

He brandished the plastic object threateningly.

"Get out of there! Hup! Hup!"

The mummy curled up into a ball.

"Don't shout so much! It's frightening him!" Angus cried.

"Who's frightening here?" Nick cried. "Get out! Scarper! Psst! Psst!"

"Stop it!" Angus screamed. And then as loud as he could, "WHAAH!"

That helped. Nick stopped and turned around.

"Can't you see you're frightening him?" Angus cried. "Just look! He's crying!"

The mummy was indeed crying. Really badly, he was sobbing his eyes out, his shoulders shaking.

"It's your fault!" Angus said angrily. "Stop being so mean!"

"Mean! That takes the biscuit," Nick said. He cautiously took a step towards the wardrobe, the ruler still raised. Then he let it drop and said, "Aw, you poor thing."

"Yes! Poor thing!" Angus said.

Nick shook his head and scratched his chin.

The most pitiful sob ever now came from the mummy.

"Do something, Dad," Angus whispered. "I can't handle it."

"Yes, I'll do something," his father said. He did nothing.

It was because he didn't know what to do, Angus understood that. But he was the oldest, so he would have to do something.

"Go on then," Angus insisted.

"Alright, erm... here, puss-puss-puss," Nick said.

"He's not a cat, Dad," Angus whispered.

"Yes, I do know that. But I have to do something, don't I? Puss-puss, come to mama. Hello, erm... boy?"

The mummy crawled even further into the corner.

Angus thought back to the Egyptian words Mr Scribble had taught them. "Enjoy your food", didn't seem very appropriate, but "MAAŞHI" meant OK. And OK was a kind word.

"Shall I have a go?" Angus pushed his father out of the way and held out his hand. "Hey, little mummy," he said. "Come on, MAAŞHI, we're friends, MAAŞHI, OK?"

To his father's astonishment, and his own too, the mummy scrambled to its feet and took his hand. Angus trembled. The bandage was rough and dirty and a brown liquid was seeping through it. And from close up, the mummy smelled disgusting, the stench was so bad his eyes began to water.

"Whumpy dumpman," Nick whispered, when the mummy stood up next to Angus. He was only a little bit smaller than Angus and he was cocking his head.

"What now, Dad?" Angus asked excitedly, as he gave his father an enquiring look.

"Erm— well done, son. Now we'll, erm—?"Nick looked just as enquiringly back.

"Go downstairs?" Angus asked.

"Yes. Downstairs," his father said.

The three of them went downstairs as though it was the most normal thing in the world. Nick went first, then the reeking little mummy and then Angus, who was pinching his nose.

In the sitting room, Angus pulled the mummy up next to him on the sofa and Nick sunk into the red chair, where he'd been sleeping a short while ago. They sat there like that for some time. Angus didn't say anything, the mummy didn't say anything and Nick sometimes opened and closed his mouth, but didn't say anything either. He had no idea what they should do, but his father would think of something.

"We need to talk to him," Nick said finally.

"How?" Angus asked.

"Like this, perhaps." Nick began to wave his arms around and gesture with his hands, but since Angus didn't have a clue what he was trying to say, there was little chance the mummy would.

"IEGH, GHRABA," the mummy said.

Nick let his arms drop. "You can say that again," he muttered.

"Maybe he could draw something, Dad," Angus suggested. He ran upstairs, fetched two pencils and a notepad and put it down on the table. He made a couple of lines on the paper and gave the other pencil to the mummy. "Now you," he said. "MAASHI. There." And when the mummy held the pencil upside down over the paper. "No, the other way round. With the point. Look, like this." He drew a figure.

"MAASHI! MAASHI!" the mummy suddenly cried. He pulled the paper towards himself and began to draw. Angus and his father looked over his shoulder in anticipation. "A straight line," Nick said. "And a triangle and a circle."

"A pyramid?" Angus said at once. "That circle is the sun. Isn't it, Dad?"

The mummy carried on drawing. A figure with black hair appeared on the paper. And then that same figure with lots of lines on it, in a box. He coloured in everything around it black.

"He's drawing himself," said Angus breathlessly. "Those lines are his bandages. And that box must be a coffin."

They carried on watching in excitement. The mummy drew a creature with six legs.

"A fly? Or a bug?" Nick suggested.

"No, wait! I know!" Angus cried. "One of those beetles! Erm, what are they called again? ... Scarabs!"

At that same moment, the mummy put his hand between his bandages and pulled something out which was hanging from a chain around his neck. Angus and his father held their breath. There was a beetle in the mummy's hand, about as big as a draughts piece. And neither of them had any doubt, the beetle was pure gold.

"A golden scarab," Angus whispered. "Dad, it really is, I'm sure. Mr Scribble told us about them. Blasting cackdingle, may I...? He reached out his hand, but the mummy shook his head violently and put the scarab back into his bandages. He picked up the pencil and carried on drawing.

A box again, this time with the scarab in it. And up above it a lightning strike which ended right on top of the beetle. And then a lot of flames. And then a running figure.

"Lightning is striking the scarab," Angus said. "There was a storm today, wasn't there? Could that be it, Dad? That he got hit by lightning and then he could run all of a sudden?"

His father just stood there shaking his head and scratching his chin, but Angus was convinced he was right.

The mummy put the pencil down and said, "DARWISHI UR-ATUM MSAMAKI MINKABH ISHAQ EBONI."

"Salad bowl, fruit pie, electric drill," Nick said. Angus burst out laughing.

The mummy pointed to his stomach. "DARWISHI UR-ATUM MSAMAKI MINKABH ISHAQ EBONI. DARWISHI UR-ATUM MSAMAKI MINKABH ISHAQ EBONI."

"Perhaps he's thirsty?" Angus suggested.

"Or he needs the loo," his father said. "What is he going on about?"

"No! It's his name! That's why he's pointing at himself!" Angus cried. "He's saying his name!"

The mummy kept on saying the same thing and pointing at himself and Nick nodded in admiration. "You're right, son," he said. "That's his name."

"Then we'll do that too, Dad. Me Angus. Angus. Angus," and Angus pointed to himself.

"Engis," the mummy said.

"And I'm Nick," said Nick.

"Nip," the mummy said, and then again, "DARWISHI UR-ATUM MSAMAKI MINKABH ISHAQ EBONI."

Angus quickly tried to write it down. It took him four attempts. "DARWISHI UR-ATUM MSAMAKI MINKABH ISHAQ EBONI," he read out.

The mummy nodded seriously.

"DARWISHI URMAKI, erm, thingy," Nick practiced. "What a name!"

Angus looked at his notepad again. And then he blurted out, "DUMMIE."

"Dummy?" his father repeated.

"Yes, Dummie! If you take all the first letters of his name, you get Dummie. Then you can say all of his names at once. You'll be able to remember that, won't you, Dad? Shall we call him that?"

"Call him? Why do we have to call him something?"

"He needs a name, doesn't he? And the other one is too difficult, you said so yourself. We'll call him Dummie. Dummie the mummy.

"DARWISHI UR-ATUM MSAMAKI MINKABH ISHAQ EBONI," the mummy said.

"No, Dummie." Angus said. "Repeat after me: Dummie. MAASHI? Dummie?"

"Dummie. Dummie. Dummie," the mummy said.

"Unbelievable," Nick said with a sigh. He got up.

"Where are you going?" Angus asked, suddenly nervous.

"I'm going to open a window," his father said. "It's too much."

Nick opened the window and looked at Angus as though the world was suddenly spinning in the opposite direction, and he didn't know what to do about it. Then he began to pace up and down.

"Angus" he began, "I've seen a lot in my life. There are lots of strange things in the world and I'm not averse to new experiences."

Angus nodded.

"But this is just not possible. Living mummies don't exist. That's weirder than growing tulips out of your ears or seeing cows rowing across the pond, or something like that."

Angus nodded.

"But it is real, because he's sitting here on our sofa and reeking so horribly my nose can't have invented it. He has made some drawings and we know what he is called."

Angus nodded for the third time. He knew what his father was doing. He was going through all the points one by one and then he would think and then he'd come up with a solution. It's what he always did. Angus looked at him expectantly. But today there was no solution because Nick asked, "What are we going to do, then?"

Angus was a little worried. Didn't his father always know everything? And if his father didn't know, how could he? "Erm, do we need to call someone?" he asked.

"I thought of that too," Nick said. "But who? The police? Fire brigade? A museum?"

"Something like that," Angus said. "They'll know what to do, won't they?"

"Maybe. But imagine calling the police and saying there's a mummy in your house. What are they going to do?"

"Think you're mad? But when they come, they'll see it's true."

"Yes, but after that?" Nick asked. "What happens next? They aren't going to say "finders keepers". No, they'll just take him away. And then— Well, think, son. A living mummy. All those people, the ones who usually poke around in dead things, are going to get their hands on a living mummy. They aren't going to play checkers with him, are they? They used to put things like that in cages, like monkeys. People used to have to pay to look at a thing like that, and feed it bananas and so on. But now—"

"What now?" Angus asked, suddenly very worried.

"They'll investigate him, of course," Nick cried. "Do experiments on him. Stick needles into him, tubes in his nose, saw his skull open, that kind of thing."

"No!" Angus cried out in disgust. "I don't want that!" He found the idea so terrible it gave him goose bumps.

"Well, me neither," his father said.

"Then let's not call anyone!" Angus pleaded.

"No. We won't call anyone."

It was quiet again for a while. Angus and Nick were both thinking the same thing: if they didn't call anyone, Dummie would stay with them.

"Shall we just hide him then?" Angus asked. "Then he can live here and we won't tell anyone."

"Someone is bound to find out," Nick said, shaking his head. "What's more, he does come from somewhere. Someone will miss him. Maybe they are looking for him. If we hide him, effectively we'll be stealing him. We could be arrested for that."

"How do you steal a person?"

"Well, kidnap them then."

"But he came to us on his own! All we did was find him."

"Who on earth finds a living mummy? They don't even exist!" Nick began to pace again. Dummie was still sitting on the sofa, not moving, not speaking.

"How about telling people he's a guest? Is that alright?" Angus volunteered. "We can say he's a relative and he was burned in an accident and now he's bandaged up. He's our cousin once removed of an aunt twice removed, or something like that." He was beginning to think this was a good idea. "And his parents were burned too, that's why they can't look after him. And then we can adopt him. Hey, then I'll have a little brother!"

"A little brother?" Angus groaned. He paced up again once more and then stopped. He hadn't been able to come up with a better plan because he said, "Alright. Alright. There isn't any other solution. He'll just have to stay."

Angus jumped up and down and mainly thought "Hooray! He's staying!" but looking at his face, his father was thinking more like: how in heavens name are we going to deal with this?

"Just for a while, eh? Until we have a better plan," Nick said. "And we'll consider a visit."

When they'd decided that Dummie would stay and that they'd call it "a visit', Nick went outside for a breath of fresh air. Angus needed one too by now, but he didn't want to leave Dummie on his own. He might run away and end up being chased by a scientist with a saw!

When his father returned, it turned out that the fresh, clean air had put a rather unsavoury thought into his head because he said, "I want to see his face now." He said it with such determination that there was no way it wasn't going to happen. Angus didn't understand. Why would his father want to see anything as disgusting as a face that had been dead for four thousand years? There might be maggots under the bandage!

"Then I can see what he's thinking," Nick explained. "I can see that with you too. Your face is saying "Don't Dad or I'll throw up", at the moment. I'm right aren't I?"

Angus nodded.

"You see. A face says everything. I want to see his eyes. I want to see if he's angry or smiling."

"But... what if he doesn't have a face anymore?" a worried Angus asked.

"Then I want to see that," his father said. He glanced outside where the rain was still pouring down. "Just a pity we can't do it in the garden," he said, pinching his nose.

"Put him under the extractor fan, Dad," Angus said. He meant it as a joke but his father's face brightened. "Good idea, son. Let's go to the kitchen."

So they went to the kitchen. Nick picked up

Dummie and set him on the counter and turned on the fan. The idea wasn't as good as it had seemed because as soon as the fan began to roar, Dummie almost fell off in fright and began to squeal like a stuck pig.

"Calm. Calm now!" Nick quickly turned off the extractor fan and held on to Dummie tightly. Dummie looked up. All of a sudden he gave the fan a hard whack.

"ѕIRѕAR!" he hissed.

"Hey," Nick cried in surprise.

"He hit my radio too, Dad," Angus said.

"What a hothead," Nick said. "Calm down now, we'll do it without the extractor fan."

Finally Dummie was calm again. Nick picked up a pair of scissors and begin to cut.

Dummie sat very, very still and that was very sensible, because Nick could be clumsy and there was a chance he might accidentally cut off Dummie's nose. If he had one, that was. But Nick was very careful. He cut off a square section of bandage. Underneath it was more bandage and Nick cut the next layer away as well. And another layer.

Angus watched breathlessly. Finally his father reached the last layer. "Tweezers," he said, as though he was a surgeon and Angus the scrub nurse. Angus quickly got the tweezers out of the first aid kit and his father used them to grasp the final strip.

"Alright, here we go," he said. "Maybe it won't be as bad as all that." Then he lifted up the last flap.

It was as bad as all that. They scared themselves to death.

"Whumpy dumpman, he'll never get a girlfriend," Nick whispered.

"Disgusting," Angus shuddered.

Dummie's skin was as brown as poo. It was dry and had cracks in it and it was pulled tight over his bones. There was a ragged hole where his nose should be and his lips were all crusty and scabby. Some of his eyelashes were stuck together, but Angus could see his eyes clearly. They were possibly the worst thing. It looked like light was coming from them, golden light, like two glowing, golden balls. Dummie could easily get a job in a haunted house, Angus thought. He felt a bit sick and looked down at the floor.

"No. Keep looking," his father instructed him.

"Why?"

"To get used to it. Remember when Bello turned up? He looked like a monster and he was covered in fleas. But he was really sweet and he stayed with us for three months. After a day, we'd already forgotten how ugly he was, do you remember?"

Of course Angus remembered. He had loved having Bello on his lap and he'd cried his eyes out when the dog disappeared suddenly.

"That means you can get used to how someone looks," Nick said. "It's much worse if someone's rotten inside."

Angus wanted to say that Dummie was probably more rotten inside than anyone else, but decided not to. Instead, he tried to carry on looking without throwing up.

"Now I'm going to try an experiment," Nick said. He bent his head towards the dirty, brown face and smiled.

Then something wild happened. Or rather, something great. Dummie's mouth got wider and a few brown teeth appeared between his crusty lips.

"He's smiling back!" Nick cried excitedly. "See that, Angus? He's smiling!"

Angus was more focussed on the fact that Dummie's lips were tearing and that he needed to brush his teeth, but apart from that his father was right. Dummie was smiling.

Nick carried on. He stuck out his tongue and out of Dummie's mouth came a strip of brown leather. He raised his eyebrows and Dummie did the same. He poked out his chin and pulled up his nose. Angus thought that unkind, because Dummie didn't have a nose. Suddenly his father pulled the angriest face he could. Dummie was so startled he almost fell off the counter. Nick quickly smiled again. And Dummie smiled back.

"It works!" cried Nick, as though he'd just repaired a washing machine and all the programmes were working again.

"You're so clever, Dad," Angus whispered.

"I agree," his father said, equally proud of himself. "And I think Dummie should keep the bandages off his face from now on. Wait a sec."

He went to the hall and returned with a mirror.

"No way—" Angus spluttered.

"Yes, he has to get used to it too," Nick said. Then he held the mirror up to Dummie's face. Dummie slapped his hand to his mouth and stood stock-still staring at himself for at least a minute. Then all of a sudden he began to pull funny faces. The brown layers of skin began to rub against his bones and he became even uglier than he already was.

"That's enough," Nick said. Then they had to go and sit facing each other in the sitting room to get used to each other.

"All three of us have freaked each other out as much as we can," Nick said, after half an hour. Angus wasn't quite sure about that, but fine.

Nick got an old sheet and cut a square section from it. He cut out two small holes at the top of the square. Then he got a Velcro strip out of the sewing box. "Sew this on, will you," he said to Angus.

Angus could do this because he did all the sewing. His father's hands were too big for it. Angus could sew on buttons and even repair a tear in a trouser leg. So he sewed the Velcro strips on to the square and more strips onto Dummie's head. Dummie didn't seem to mind. Angus did though, because he had to sit with his own face really close to the haunted house face all that time. But he got used to it much faster that way. Only the smell was really terrible.

When Angus had finished, his father pressed the fabric to Dummie's face and studied him from a distance.

"Angus, son, we're good at this," he said contentedly.

Dummie picked up the mirror and lifted up the white square with his other hand, and then put it back again.

"MAASHI," he said. Evidently he thought they were good too.

"What now?" Angus asked.

"Now it's very late. We're going to make up a guest bed," his father said. "Dummie, you're going to have a sleep!"

"Sheep," Dummie said.

"Can he sleep in my room?" Angus asked at once.

"Of course," his father said.

They went upstairs, Nick made up the camp bed and opened the window. Then he sat down on Angus' bed, rubbed his chin and looked at Angus. Angus looked back and decided they were both thinking the same thing. That they didn't have a clue what was happening.

"Is Dummie going to stay with us forever now? Angus asked.

"I have no idea," his father replied.

"But he can't go anywhere else, can he? That thing you said about the people who do experiments and stuff..."

Nick wrapped his arm around Angus' shoulders.

"We won't let that happen, son. We'll just see how things go. And you need to sleep. And he does too, by the way. And tomorrow, we'll start off by dealing with that smell."

Then he left them alone.

Of course Angus couldn't sleep. And not only because he was lying next to a stink bomb. How can you sleep after experiencing something like this? His mind was bursting with questions. Where did Dummie come from, for example? And would he still be there tomorrow? And would Angus be able to keep it to himself? And what would they do if anyone saw Dummie? And his father had said that they'd actually kidnapped him, so they might be criminals now too. All of a sudden he had a very big secret.

Dummie was lying on his back. He had got his scarab out of his bandages and was slowly turning it around. When he saw Angus looking, he suddenly held out his hand. "MAASHI," he said. MAASHI? Did he mean that Angus could touch the scarab? Angus carefully reached out his hand. And then he was allowed to hold the scarab for a while.

The object was cold and as heavy as a rock. Angus had expected to feel something else as well, a strange power perhaps. But he didn't. He returned the scarab and Dummie put it back safely under his bandages. Then he looked at Angus with his golden eyes and smiled in that ghoulish way. Angus suddenly felt warm inside. The most wretched boy in the whole world was lying next to him. And he had let him touch his most

valuable possession and he was smiling at him. Angus
smiled back. How lucky that Dummie had come to
their house, he thought. His father would take good
care of him, and he would too.

Dummie muttered something he couldn't
understand, rolled over and pulled the covers over his
head.

CHAPTER 2

A special weekend

The next day was Saturday. Angus and his father always had a lie-in on Saturday mornings, but today they didn't get a chance. Angus was woken up by blaring music. He blinked his eyes and immediately smelled that horrible smell. Dead mice? Dummie!

Angus shot up in bed. Dummie was sitting at his desk hitting the radio. Music – nothing – different music – nothing –

"Hey, you'll break it! Dummie! Don't do that!"

Dummie grinned and gave the radio another smack

and then began to jig his chest in time to the music. It looked quite funny but Dummie kept on hitting the radio, so Angus took it off him and put it in his cupboard. "No!" he said in a strict voice.

Suddenly he heard shouting.

"Angus! ANGUS!"

What was going on now? Angus ran downstairs with Dummie right behind him.

Nick was standing in the hall holding the newspaper and pointing excitedly at an article. "It's in here! I know where he comes from! Listen to this." He began to read:

"Yesterday's storms left a trail of destruction across the country. An exceptional number of trees and overhead wires were struck by lightning. On the A13 near Polderdam, lightning hit a truck. The driver lost control of the vehicle and drove through the crash barrier down an embankment where the truck burst into flames. The truck was unsalvageable. It is miraculous that the driver escaped with only superficial injuries, although he is still being treated for shock."

"What do they mean, shock?" Angus asked.
"That he had a fright and he's still feeling confused," Nick explained. He continued to read.

"The truck was transporting three ancient sarcophagi containing three mummies. Only the scorched remains were found. This is a great setback for The Grobbe Museum, which was their destination. One of the mummies was a pharaoh, the other was an unknown woman. The third mummy was a child. This loss is the greatest, since the miniature mummy was unusually intact."

"What's "intact"?" Angus asked.
"That he's still whole," his father said.
Angus looked at the ragged hole in Dummie's face where his nose had once been. He wasn't that intact.

Nick lowered the newspaper and showed the picture of the burning truck. There was a cry from behind them. Dummie had seen it too and was pointing excitedly at the picture.

"Look! He recognises it too," Nick said. "Well, now we know for sure. Dummie was in that truck. And do you know what that means, Angus? That nobody is looking for him! Dummie was burned. Dead and burned. Great. We don't have to worry about that anymore." He walked over to his computer and turned it on. It was old and didn't always work, but thankfully it didn't give him any trouble today. "I'm going to look up The Grobbe Museum, son," Nick said. He concentrated on the screen. "Yes. Here it is! An exhibition of three mummies from the National Museum of Antiquities was going to open this week. There isn't anything about the accident. And nothing about the mummies either, for that matter."

"Why don't you look for that other museum, Dad?" Angus suggested.

His father looked up the National Museum of Antiquities and a few seconds later they were staring in amazement at a picture of Dummie. "There, the fourth one along. That's him!" Nick sunk back into his chair. "Unbelievable," he said.

Angus studied the row of mummies in coffins on the screen. The fourth one was definitely Dummie. Angus clicked on the photo and read: *Unknown mummy of a boy, between eight and ten years of age. Probably from the firth or sixth dynasty. Found in a small grave during excavations around Gizeh in 1957 and acquired by the National Museum in 2002.*

Dummie stared at the screen, wide-eyed. He ran to the mirror and back again three times.

"Dummie!" he cried excitedly. "Dummie! Dummie!"

Nick ran a wider search but didn't find any other pictures or information.

"We still don't know very much, Dad," Angus said disappointedly.

"What did you want to know then?" Nick asked.

"You know. Where he comes from."

"From somewhere near Gizeh. It says so here."

"Yes, but what I really mean is: who was he?"

"Only he knows that. Maybe he will be able to tell us something about it later. But even so, it doesn't make the slightest bit of difference. Even if we know exactly where he comes from and how old he is. Even if we know what he ate before he died. He is and will remain a lost and homeless mummy."

Dummie continued to stare at the screen.

"We can also show him things from Egypt, Dad," Angus said. "Maybe he'll recognise something."

"Let's wait a bit with that," said Nick as he turned off the computer. Dummie shouted something and quickly pressed on the button again.

"No!" said Nick.

Dummie reached out and gave the computer a whack. "ꜱ I R ꜱ A R!" he hissed.

"Stop it, you hothead!" Nick said. He pushed his chair back and secretly pulled the plug out of the socket. "Let's have breakfast first," he said.

So they had breakfast. That's to say, Angus and his father had breakfast. Because one of the first things they discovered was that Dummie didn't eat.

Nick had moved the kitchen table towards the open window and had got out three plates, three cups and three knives. Angus put all the spreads on the table. Butter, chocolate spread, peanut butter, honey, pâté and cheese.

"Alright. First honey then," Nick said.
He spread honey on half a slice of bread and put it on Dummie's plate. "What was that thing for enjoy your food again?"

"BIL HENNAH IL SHIFFA," Angus said.
"Alright. BIL HENNAH, erm... stuff," Nick said
Dummie took a big bite. Angus and his father watched Dummie's face expectantly. A bit of sludge oozed from Dummie's mouth and his skin stretched worryingly tight over his bones. Next thing his teeth fall out, Angus thought.

"That's good, he likes it," Nick said happily.

"ʙʟᴇɢʜ!" said Dummie at that same instant. He gagged and spat up a mouthful of brown sludge onto the tablecloth.

"Strewth," Nick said in dismay. He pulled a face and cleared it up. Then he spread the other half of the slice with peanut butter. But that came back out again half-digested too after a few seconds. "Strewth!" Nick cried again. Dummie gave up. When Nick offered him a dry slice of bread, he shook his head. Nothing more passed his lips.

"He has to eat. If he doesn't eat, he'll die," said Nick anxiously.

"He's already dead," Angus said. "And hang on, perhaps he doesn't have a stomach anymore!" He knew that kind of thing from the Egypt competition, that they took the stomach and intestines out of the mummies sometimes.

"Now you're teaching me something," his father said with sudden relief. "Well, that should solve another problem."

"Which one?"

"Then he doesn't need to poo," Nick chuckled.

"To poo?" Angus roared with laughter. And his father did too, and because they were laughing, Dummie joined in. "ᴍᴀᴀꜱʜɪ! ᴍᴀᴀꜱʜɪ!" he cried. Then they couldn't stop laughing and neither could Dummie. He laughed his head off and looked terrible, with his crooked, open mouth full of brown teeth and bits of peanut butter.

"What a sight!" Nick howled.

"Horrible," Angus hiccupped.

"MAASHI!" cried Dummie.

Finally they stopped laughing. Angus looked at his jam sandwich and glass of milk. "Shall we give him a bath first?" he wondered.

"Good idea," his father said. "I'll go up and run it."

When Angus had finished his sandwich, he took Dummie to the bathroom. His father must have added a whole bottle of bubble bath because the foam came right up to the rim. Dummie gave the white stuff a suspicious look.

"Shouldn't he erm... get undressed?" Angus asked.

Nick didn't think so. "Those strips are completely stuck to his skin," he said. "We'll just duck him, bandages and all." But Dummie wasn't having any of it. When Nick picked him up to put him in the water, he began to scream like a stuck pig.

"Whumpy dumpman," Nick grumbled. "It's only water, you know."

But because Dummie just screamed harder, he put him back down. Dummie raced out of the bathroom. Angus ran after him and found him in the cupboard under the stairs, crouching next to the phone book shaking.

"MAASHI?" Angus asked.

Dummie shook his head.

"You stink, man," Angus cried. "You need to have a bath. MAASHI! Now."

He could just as well have been talking to the phone book, because Dummie refused to come out of the cupboard. Nick came downstairs, took one look at the shaking wreck and decided that a bath wasn't such a good idea. "Then we'll just wash the outside," he said.

He filled a bucket and dragged Dummie along with him. Angus and his father rubbed green soap all over him and carefully patted him dry. Dummie protested strongly: he really didn't like water. But Nick firmly insisted, he wasn't going to spend the rest of his life sitting next to a carton of rotten eggs, he said. Finally they were done. They put Dummie on a chair in the sun and Angus sat down next to him.

"Sit," said Angus.

"Shit," said Dummie.

Angus gave Dummie a stunned look, stood up and sat down again. "Stand, sit," he said.

Dummie followed suit. "Shtand, shit," he repeated.

Blasting cackdingle, Angus thought. I taught two words to a mummy! Full of excitement, he quickly taught him some more words. Lie down, grass, house, shed. He thought about the trouble with his radio this morning and taught him the word "no".

In the meantime, Nick hung up the washing. It was windy and the sheets flapped in the wind. When he finished, he walked over to Dummie with a smile. Before Dummie knew what had hit him, he'd picked him up and put him on top of the rotary dryer.

"Sit still now, little guy," Nick said happily.

That was unlikely. Dummie crawled along a pole to the edge of the dryer and then hung from it like it was a climbing frame. He began to swing back and forth wildly, shouting out all the words Angus had taught him. "Shtand! Shit! Ghrass! Ghouse!"

"What a lot of energy. You can see he's slept for a few thousand years," Nick joked. When Dummie hung himself upside down, Angus and his father laughed their socks off, until the dryer toppled over and Dummie and the clean wash ended up on the ground.

"Whumpy dumpman," Nick said in dismay.

Angus got the giggles again, and while he lay there in stitches, his father picked up the sheets to put them back in the washing machine and a contented Dummie returned to sitting in the sun. "Shit," he said.

By the time Nick returned a second time to hang the sheets (this time on an old bit of washing line), Dummie was dry.

Unfortunately washing him had not helped much. Dummie did look a little cleaner than before, but he stank just as badly.

"It's coming from the inside," Nick said. "We'll have to disguise that. We'll have to coat him in something that smells more than he does." He walked off and returned with his hands full of bottles and sprays. "Here. Aftershave. Deodorant. Extra strong toilet freshener. Lemon juice."

"Lemon juice?"

"I like the smell of it. Come on, let's experiment."

Angus and his father sprayed different smells onto small strips of bandage and sniffed. The thing that worked best was a heavy dose of toilet freshener. They ended up spraying Dummie from head to foot in it. Now Dummie no longer stank of rotten eggs but like the toilet after his father had just used it, Angus thought.

By now it was nearly eleven o'clock. Nick decided they should just have a normal day. He said, "We'll pretend we've just got a new kitten. You'd have to teach it a few things: where the food bowl is, that it needs to use the litter tray, that it mustn't scratch."

Angus didn't think this was a good comparison. Dummie didn't eat, didn't go to the toilet and his fingernails were bandaged up. And Dummie didn't just need to learn a few things, but everything.

Then Nick said something good. He said, "I think it's a job for you, Angus. You show Dummie the ropes and get him used to this century, and I'll go do the shopping. You can do that, can't you?"

"Yes, of course I can!" Angus replied at once. And as his father walked to the car, he took Dummie back inside. He look around hesitantly. Showing Dummie the ropes in the twenty-first century was quite a big job. Where on earth should he start?

He decided to take him around the whole house and point at things and say the word for them. So he started off, "Wall. Door. Window. Stairs. Curtains. Bed. Cupboard. Towel." He skipped the bathroom before Dummie ended up in the cupboard again. They went back downstairs and into the kitchen. "Kitchen," Angus said. "Tap. Fridge. Pan. Frying pan. Saucepan." He opened the cutlery drawer. "Fork. Knife." He looked at the spoons. It wasn't normal to have that many different kinds. "Soup spoon, teaspoon, desert spoon, serving spoon, gravy spoon, ladle." He closed the drawer again. There was no end to it. If he had to name everything, they'd still be going tomorrow.

Dummie was happy to go along with everything. He politely followed Angus around, listened carefully and repeated everything. He remembered quite a lot too, Angus noticed when he took him on a second tour of the house. After the third round, Dummie had had enough. And Angus had too. They ended up back in the kitchen.

Angus got out a cup and turned on the tap. Dummie stared at the water coming out of the small object in disbelief. "Good, isn't it?" Angus smiled. "I can do magic." He took a sip and saw Dummie giving the extractor fan a suspicious look. Aha. He would have to show Dummie right away that the fan wasn't dangerous. He quickly turned it on and off a few times. Dummie jumped back, but when he understood that the thing wasn't going to attack him, he wanted to have a go himself. He kept on pressing the button until Angus finally said, "Enough!" and pulled him away. But Dummie had given Angus a good idea: if he showed Dummie all the switches in the house, he could press them a few times and the novelty would wear off.

"Come with me," he said, because Dummie understood those words by now.

He went to the sitting room and turned all the lights on and off. "Light," he said proudly, as though he was making it himself. He let Dummie play with the switches for a bit and then took him to see the doorbell. Angus pressed it and Dummie copied. First carefully, but the second time he wouldn't take his finger off again. *Trrrrring!* It went for a whole minute. This was why Angus didn't hear the postman until he was already in the garden.

"Good morning!" he heard all of a sudden. Angus spun round and nearly jumped out of his skin. He pushed Dummie indoors and slammed the door shut at the same time. The postman was probably still half-asleep because he just gave the post to Angus, turned around and walked off whistling.

Angus breathed a sigh of relief. That was stupid, no one was allowed to see Dummie and it had nearly gone wrong already. He quickly rang the doorbell but it no longer worked. Dummie must have broken it.

He went round the back and in through the kitchen door and saw Dummie pressing the button on the extractor fan. "Don't!" he cried. Dummie laughed and gestured that Angus should carry on with his magic tricks. Angus began to grin. Well, he'd impress Dummie now!

He got two slices of bread and put them in the toaster and pushed them down. He reached out a hand and pretended to mutter some secret words. Dummie looked at the glowing elements with curiosity. Angus chuckled. Not long now...

FLOOP! The slices of toast jumped right up into Dummie's face.

"ꗸIRꗸAꗸ!" Dummie cried out in shock and Angus roared with laughter. Dummie angrily picked up the two slices of toast, put them back in the toaster and pushed it down again. Soon nasty smoke was coming from the appliance. Angus pushed Dummie aside and tried to get the blackened slices of toast out of the toaster. FLOOP! This time they hit him on the nose and Dummie roared. "MAASHI! MAASHI!" he cried.

"Alright. Now we're even," Angus giggled. He filled a soup bowl with water, got the mixer and dipped it in. "Here, hold tight," he said.

Dummie mixed and mixed. "Zoom zoom!" he sung as he rocked back and forth in time. "Zoom! Zoom!" His dancing became wilder. "ZOOM! ZOOM!" BAM! The bowl tumbled from the counter and shattered into a thousand pieces. Dummie waved the

mixer around in shock. "Hey! Look out!" Angus just had time to shout. But it was too late. The mixer hit Dummie's leg and suddenly all bits of bandage were flying around. As fast as he could, Angus pulled the plug from the socket. He looked in dread at Dummie's thigh, where the bandage had come off. The leg was as brown as Dummie's face. There were tears in the skin and Angus could even see a bit of dark brown bone between the stringy bits of dried flesh. Dummie looked at his own leg with interest, stuck his tongue out and pulled a horrified expression. Angus quickly unravelled the bandage from the mixer and tied it around Dummie's leg again as best he could. It wouldn't hold though, so Angus got a new bandage from the first aid kit. He tied that around the old one and finished it off with a few sticking plasters. In the meantime, he couldn't get his head around the fact that Dummie hadn't felt anything. Maybe Dummie wouldn't even feel it if you stuck a pin in him.

When everything was back in place, Angus mopped the floor with a sponge and fetched the vacuum cleaner. Dummie was impressed by the new object. He knelt down and watched fascinated as the bits of broken bowl flew into the hose, one by one. "Good, isn't it?" Angus chuckled. "bits on the floor, bits in the vac— No! Don't!"

But Dummie had put his hand in front of the hose and now it had latched onto him. "SIRSAR!" he screamed as he kicked the vacuum cleaner as hard as he could. Angus turned it off and Dummie was free again. To Angus' horror there was now a whole length of bandage missing from Dummie's hand. It looked as awful as his leg. And it was much more difficult to repair!

Angus shook as he counted Dummie's fingers. Five, thank god. He opened the vacuum cleaner, got out the bandage and wrapped up all the fingers again.

Angus thought it would be safest to just go and watch television now. He had wanted to show Dummie the gas oven as a crowning touch, but maybe his new friend was too clumsy for that. He'd just escaped from a burning truck, he mustn't go up in flames in the kitchen!

The television was a good idea. Dummie thought it was the most amazing thing so far. He kept on pointing to all the people and animals and buildings which all seemed to be in that cupboard. When Nick returned half an hour later with the shopping, Dummie was still glued to the set, his golden eyes staring.

"Everything OK?" Nick asked.

"Great," Angus replied.

"Berry ghood," repeated Dummie without looking up.

"What's that then?" Nick pointed at Dummie's leg.

Angus blushed. "Nothing. Well, we had a little accident. Dummie banged his leg and then a bit of the bandage came off. So I fixed it up a bit."

"Banged his leg? On what?" his father asked.

"Nothing much. Well, on the mixer," Angus mumbled, as he turned even redder.

"The mixer? How do you bang yourself on a mixer?!" Nick cried.

"I had to show it to him, didn't I? It's something from this century! But the postman didn't see Dummie. And Dummie thinks everything is weird," Angus rattled on. "Even normal things, like water from the tap, and the lights and so on."

Luckily his father began to laugh. "Fine. Then you can learn something from him too," he said. "Things like that aren't normal."

Angus thought this was nonsense, because water from a tap was normal and so was light. His father had never said anything about it before. But he'd better agree with him for now.

Nick left Angus and Dummie on their own for the rest of the afternoon. Maybe he's doing it deliberately, thought Angus. In any case, his father wasn't painting because he came to check on them from time to time and there wasn't any paint on his trousers. Sometimes he tapped on the window and made a circle with his thumb and index finger. That meant he thought it was going well. And that made Angus very happy.

It was late when Angus and his father sat down to dinner. They ate bread with fried eggs and the left-over broccoli. Dummie, of course, didn't eat anything.

After dinner they made an important discovery.

It started with an idea of Nick's. He'd just cleared the table and was sitting on his red chair to have a thirty minute nap, but it wasn't working and suddenly he jumped up. "Shall we go to the place the accident happened?" he asked.

"With the truck? Why?" Angus asked.

"You know. Just to see. I can't sleep. I just want to see it."

"What about Dummie?"

"He'll come with us. Maybe he'd like to see it too. And we can't leave him here on his own."

So they wrapped Dummie up in an enormous raincoat and put a hat on him. Angus found an old pair of trainers for him and then they were ready.

They got into the car and Dummie had to sit on the backseat under a blanket. Angus sat next to him and Nick started up the engine. Dummie began to scream in terror. Angus said "MAASHI" at least a hundred times and rubbed Dummie's shoulders until he finally sat still. After a while, Dummie's head came out from under the blanket and he peered outside cautiously. It wasn't long before he began to babble and point excitedly.

First Nick drove along the motorway, past the place where the truck had gone through the crash barrier. Then he took a turn and drove back along a quiet lane. He parked the car on the verge and they had to walk for a bit. It had grown dark in the meantime and Nick held onto Dummie's hand tightly. "There it is, next to the red and white tape," he said. "Hang on." He took a good look around. "Alright. I can't see anyone. Follow me."

The site of the accident was deserted. The truck had been towed away and everything had been cleared up. All they could see were a load of tyre tracks, a burned, toppled tree and the red and white tape. Dummie pointed at the tree excitedly and to a shallow ditch. He kept shouting out and it was obvious he recognised the place. But they already knew that this was where he had come from.

"What's that?" Angus asked all of a sudden. He pointed at two white lights getting increasingly closer.

"Huh? That's a car. Quick, hide!" Nick called out.

Angus grabbed Dummie by the hand and dived into the ditch with him. He pressed Dummie to the ground and crawled as best he could under the gigantic raincoat. "Shhh!" he hissed. Cautiously, he peered out over the edge.

The car drove right across the field towards them and stopped near the tree. A man got out. He was tall and broad and had a full head of messy curls.

Angus heard his father start talking enthusiastically to the man. "Good evening. Did you just want to have a look at the accident too?"

"Yes, something like that," the man said in a deep voice. "I was driving the truck. I just wanted to come back and check something."

"Oh. You were the driver, weren't you? I read about it in the paper. You must have been in terrible shock."

"Well, not just from the accident. I thought I saw something yesterday. In that ditch. I'm not sure."

"What did you see?" Nick asked.

"A mummy. There were mummies in my truck. And I think I saw one crawl out of that ditch."

Angus froze. But to his astonishment his father began to laugh. "A living mummy? They don't exist," he chuckled.

"No. But I'm not mad, am I?" the man said.

"Well, why don't you have a good look in the ditch," Nick said.

In the ditch? How could his father say that!

"And what are you doing here, exactly?" the man asked, suddenly suspicious.

"Oh, you know, simple curiosity," Nick said. "I live nearby and wanted to take a look. People are like that, aren't they? Crazy about accidents. But there's nothing to see. Everything has been cleared up. Except perhaps that mummy in the ditch. Wait, I'll come with you. You look here, and I'll look over there."

To his horror, Angus heard heavy footsteps approaching. He wrapped his arm around Dummie, made himself even smaller and held his breath. Through the fabric of the coat he saw the light of a torch go past. "Nothing here," his father's voice said above him. "What about over there?"

"Nothing either, of course," the man muttered, a short way off.

"Well, then you must have been mistaken," Nick said. "Quite possible, eh? Shock of it all."

"Yes, from the shock. The policemen said so too."

Angus heard his father walking away and breathed again. Nick and the man carried on talking a little further up. Then a car engine started and after that it went quiet again.

"Angus, Dummie, are you still there?" Nick called out quietly.

"No, I'm as dead as Dummie," Angus groaned. "Will you promise never to do anything like that again?" He got up, and reached down to pull Dummie to his feet. Then he spotted it. It was half under Dummie's foot by a clump of grass and it was small, square-shaped and bright green. They'd probably been lying on top of it. "What's that?" he asked. He bent down, picked it up and held it up to his nose. It was a tiny, green book with crumpled brown pages. It was wet, but he could see the doodles on it quite clearly.

Doodles? No, these weren't doodles! These were hieroglyphics! "Dad!" he shouted excitedly. "DAD!" He turned around but before he could take a step, Dummie grabbed the book from his hands. He leafed through it eagerly.

"GHEPSETSUT! GHEPSETSUT!" he cried out and then he pushed it between his bandages.

"What was that?" Nick asked in surprise.

"A book! With hieroglyphics! It must be Dummie's. He must have lost it yesterday. Let's go home, Dad, he might let us look at it!"

"Yes. No. Wait a minute, perhaps there's more here," Nick said.

They searched the ditch together. But they didn't find anything else.

"Alright. Let's go," Nick said. Soon they were driving home in silence.

Back at the house, Dummie got the book out from under his bandages and allowed Angus and his father to hold it. There was a picture of the scarab on the first page. And there were more pictures on the pages following it. A cat, a falcon and a sun. Apart from that, it was indeed full of hieroglyphics.

"Wow," Nick said. "So. Well." He didn't understand any of it. Angus thought that was quite normal, because hieroglyphics were just as extinct as dinosaurs.

"Shall we look them up?" Angus suggested. "Maybe there's something useful in here. Where he's from, perhaps. Right, Dad? And Dummie said GEPSETSUT or something. What could that be?"

Nick turned on the computer and looked up hieroglyphics. There were all kinds of hieroglyphics from different periods. They tried to compare them with those in the book but it was an endless task. Worse still, some of the hieroglyphics in the book were so small they needed a magnifying glass. By the end, they had recognized a few symbols but that was all.

"Well, alright," Nick said. "We found something of Dummie's. Great. But I can't make head nor tail of it. Nor anything sensible either, for that matter." He typed in "GEPSETSUT" and looked at the screen. "My computer asks whether we mean HEPSETSUT," he chucked. "Hang on. Yes, look here, that's an Egyptian name."

"I still think he said GEPSETSUT," Angus said.

"Then he can't pronounce the H," Nick said. "Shall we look up Dummie's name too?"

Angus got the piece of paper where he'd written down Dummie's names the previous evening and his father typed all six of them in: "DARWISHI UR-ATUM MSMAKI MINKABH ISHAQ EBONI'. Now they finally discovered that Dummie was actually called HOLY GREAT FAIR FISHY LAUGHING DARK. But they were none the wiser.

Nick turned off the computer. "Tomorrow's a new day," he said. "Both of you need to go to bed."

Dummie took the book upstairs with him and put it on the bedside table. Soon they were both under the covers. While Dummie played with his scarab, Angus picked up the book and studied the pictures. They all looked lovely and it was certainly something special. But it was no use to them at all.

They didn't wake up until nine am on Sunday. First Nick sprayed Dummie with toilet freshener and then they had breakfast.

"Listen," said Nick, when they'd finished. "You can play inside, or outside in the back garden. If you're in the back garden only a few cows will be able to see Dummie and they won't tell anyone."

"They might, but no one would understand them," Angus giggled.

Nick cleared the table and Angus got out the chessboard. He set up the pieces and began teaching Dummie how to play chess. It wasn't a great success. Dummie understood that they had to take turns and that the pieces all did something different. But when Angus took one of his pawns and put it next to the board he became cross. "ꜱɪʀꜱᴀʀ!" he cried and put the pawn back on the board.

"That's how you're supposed to play it," Angus protested. "Watch." He took Dummie's knight with his own knight and cried, "Hooray!" and clapped his hands.

Dummie instantly swept all of Angus' other pieces from the board with his other knight and shouted "Ghooray!" at least ten times. Then Angus put the chessboard back in his bedroom.

He was still upstairs when he heard an enormous scream coming from downstairs.

Angus dashed down the stairs and ran into the sitting room. Dummie had got the vacuum cleaner out of the cupboard, taken a roll of toilet paper and held the end of it to the hose. The hose was blocked and the vacuum cleaner bellowed like it was about to explode. A second later, Nick ran into the room.

"No! That's naughty!" he shouted angrily. And then he shouted "Whumpy dumpman!" just as loudly. He put the vacuum cleaner back in the hall cupboard and slammed the door behind him. "Outside, both of you! Go play on the swing or something!"

Angus looked at his father's stern expression and smiled secretly to himself. He cheerfully pulled Dummie out to the swing, which was hanging from a tree in the back garden. But Dummie had other plans. He took a running jump, grabbed onto a branch and swung himself up. He was as agile as a monkey and in no time at all he was right at the top of the tree.

"Watch out, man," Angus shouted, when Dummie began to sway back and forth. "Come down!" But Dummie swayed harder and harder from left to right. Suddenly there was a loud crack and Dummie hit the ground like a sack.

Angus was in shock. Now Dummie had broken

SMACK

all of his ribs. And his legs and arms and if he was unlucky his neck too! "Dummie!" he cried.

But Dummie just got up again, shook his head a bit and then climbed the tree again. He jumped down again, this time landing on his feet and then ran into the house. Angus followed him, non-plussed. He found Dummie in his room, when he'd got the chessboard out on Angus' bed. "Chess! Chess!" he said.

"Yeah, steady on, eh?" Angus said. He looked at Dummie, shook his head and set up the pieces.

"Angus! Hey! Angus!" a voice called.

Angus froze. That was Ebbi's voice. Ebbi? Oh no! Ebbi was coming over today to give him a book about Egypt for his homework. And he was coming up the stairs by the sound of it! Hadn't his father been able to stop him?

His eyes darted around the room. "Quick, into the wardrobe!" he said and when Dummie failed to understand, he just shoved him in. "Hey, Angus, your doorbell's broken," he laughed. "I just went round the back. I've broken in! Hands up or I'll shoot."

Angus tried to laugh but didn't quite manage it.

"Here's the book," Ebbi said. He looked at the chessboard and the extra bed in Dummie's room. "Got guests?"

"No, erm... my bed's broken. The base, I mean. And I'm playing myself," Angus said quickly.

"Oh. Who's winning then?" Ebbi giggled.

"No one. I might be. Erm... shall we go downstairs?"

All of a sudden loud music came out of the

wardrobe. Angus' heart stopped. The radio!
"What's that?" Ebbi asked in astonishment.
  "Erm... my radio," Angus said.

what's that?

"Have you got a radio in your wardrobe?"
  "No. Yes. Only today." Angus started to sweat. "It's
my alarm clock-radio. It didn't go off this morning and
now it suddenly has. I'll just turn it off." He opened
the wardrobe and checked Ebbi couldn't see around
the corner. Dummie was kneeling and rocking in
time to the music. Angus quickly turned off the radio.
Dummie shot to his feet.
  "No!" Angus whispered. "Quiet!"
  "What did you say?" Ebbi asked.

"Erm... nothing. I mean: nothing to you. I was talking to the radio. I want it to shut up." Angus closed the wardrobe door and turned around. "I talk to things sometimes. You must know that."

"Oh yeah, that's true," Ebbi chuckled. "And? Have you found anything out about mummies?"

MUMMIES?

"Mummies?" Angus' voice cracked.

"For school. Our homework."

"Oh, erm... no, not yet." To his horror, Angus saw the wardrobe door opening behind Ebbi. Whaah! He hadn't locked it! Dummie crept out of the wardrobe, looked at Ebbi's back and stuck his tongue out.

"Shall we go downstairs?" Angus asked in panic. "I'm thirsty. And we've got ice-cream. Do you want ice-cream?" Without waiting for an answer, he pushed Ebbi out of his room and down the stairs.

"Are you feeling alright?" Ebbi asked when they'd reached the bottom.

"No. I'm a bit ill. But thanks for bringing the book. See ya!"

Ebbi stayed where he was. "Well?" he asked in a questioning voice.

"Well what?"

"The ice-cream?"

"Oh, right." Angus went to the freezer. "Oh no, it's all gone," he said, trying to sound surprised.

As Ebbi gave him an even more astonished look, Angus looked out of the window and saw Dummie falling past it outside. Dummie got up, waved and walked to the shed. Angus groaned inwardly. Ebbi would have to leave now, before he had a heart attack.

"Hey, Angus, I think you are ill. You look like you've seen a ghost," Ebbi said, concerned.

"Huh? Yes. No. My father and I are off in a minute. To the zoo. Thanks so much for bringing the book."

Ebbi left at last. Angus closed the door behind him and leaned against it. He waited until his heart had stopped pounding and then ran to the shed. Nick had given Dummie a sheet of paper and he was sitting there happily drawing on it.

"Dad! Ebbi was here! I almost died of fright."

"What? Did he see Dummie?"

"No! I hid him in the wardrobe. But he turned the radio on in there and then he walked right past Ebbi's back. He didn't understand he had to hide. He doesn't listen. He just does what he wants!"

Nick scratched his chin. "We'll have to teach him to

talk as quickly as possible," he said. "Look how well he can draw, by the way. He's got real talent, that boy."

Angus looked at Dummie's drawing. "Yes. Very nice," he said. "But teach him to talk first."

The rest of the day passed without incident. No one came to call and Dummie didn't fall out of any more trees. They ate potatoes with broccoli, watched television and went to bed on time. Nick came upstairs with them and sat down on Angus' bed. "You'll just go to school as usual tomorrow," he said.

"What's Dummie going to do then?" Angus asked.

"He'll stay with me. I won't let him out of my sight. And you need to keep quiet. You mustn't tell anyone about Dummie. Will you manage it?"

Angus thought about Mr Scribble. He always knew instantly when you were hiding something. "I won't say a thing," he said.

"And if anyone sees him by accident, we'll say we have a guest who got burned in a fire, like we agreed," his father said. "Granny's sister's nephew, or something like that. Dummie's not a mummy. Will you remember all that?" He suddenly looked worried.

"Oh Dad, Dummie isn't a mummy, is he? You're just in shock, like the truck driver," Angus said as a joke.

But his father didn't laugh. "I'm aware of the facts," Nick said seriously. "They're just very strange facts."

Well, Angus couldn't deny that.

CHAPTER 3

The EarLy weeks

There was only one school in Polderdam and it was called Hobble Primary or Hobble's for short. Hobble Primary was on the edge of the village. It was a cheerful white building with red window frames and in front of it there was a large playground with a couple of playground toys for the infants and an enormous climbing frame for everyone.

Angus was in Mr Scribble's class. Mr Scribble

was the oldest teacher at Hobble's. He walked with a stoop, his face was covered in wrinkles and he wore old-fashioned clothes, like trousers with sharp creases and shirts with a stripy tie. Just like all old teachers, Mr Scribble loved books. He said he had read all the books in the library, and Angus believed him too. His teacher was like a walking computer. It didn't matter what he asked, Mr Scribble always knew the answer. He understood everybody, always wanted to help and hardly ever got angry. Angus thought Mr Scribble was the bee's knees.

Mr Scribble

Miss Frick was the headmaster at Hobble's. She was the exact opposite of Mr Scribble. She probably knew a lot too, but she was a thousand times stricter. She was upset so often that it had ruined her whole face. There were two deep folds running from the corners of her mouth right down to her chin, like a bulldog. She had sneaky green pig's eyes that saw everything (even when there was nothing to see) and when she was talking to someone, she always held her nose in the air. Then you looked right up her nostrils, which made her look just like a pig.

Miss Frick

And she had a horrible, crabby voice too. Angus hated Miss Frick. He stayed as far away from her as he could.

"Don't say anything to anyone," Nick said for the hundredth time that Monday morning.

"No, Dad, I won't say anything," Angus said for the hundredth time back.

"Don't even think about Dummie. Think about other nice things. Like getting a new kitten, or something."

"Sure, Dad. I'll think about getting a new kitten, or something," Angus said obediently.

Then his father and Dummie waved him off.

When he got to school, Angus locked his bike, walked into the classroom and told himself not to think about Dummie. Of course, this was ridiculous, because when he tried not to think about Dummie, it made him think about him.

But anyway, he managed it. Angus didn't say anything to anyone, not even to Ebbi, who asked whether he'd won his chess game yesterday.

"I didn't play anyone," Angus flashed back.

"You did," Ebbi said. "I saw it with my own eyes!"

Angus went white. "Who did I play then?"

"With yourself, you idiot!"

"Oh, yeah," Angus muttered. "Well, I won."

He couldn't concentrate that day at all and Mr Scribble asked him what he was daydreaming about three times.

"About a new kitten," Angus answered the first time.

"Nice. Have you got a new kitten?" Mr Scribble asked.

"No," Angus said. The whole class laughed.

The second time he didn't say anything, and the third time, Annalisa said he was in love. "With a new kitten," she said. That gave Lizzy a fit of giggles, at which point Mr Scribble luckily paid more attention to Lizzy than to him.

In the afternoon, Angus almost let it slip. They were allowed to work on their Egypt projects and after a while Mr Scribble looked up. "Have any of you ever seen a real mummy?" he asked.

"I haven't. I have seen a new kitten though," Angus replied without thinking.

The whole class burst out laughing again. Mr Scribble too. "That's a shame," he said. "I was planning on taking you all to The Grobbe Museum to look at real mummies, but there was a traffic accident last Friday and the mummies were burned. Well, perhaps we'll go to the National Museum. At least, if I can get Miss Frick to agree."

"Yes, great," Angus said. He looked at his exercise book and Mr Scribble picked up a text book. Phew. Keeping a secret took lots of skill.

At last it was three o'clock and the bell went. Angus sprang onto his bike and raced home.

Dummie was sitting in the shed, drawing with Angus' father. He jumped to his feet when he saw Angus.

"Hangus! Hangus! Ghooray!" he cried.

"Dummie!" Angus cried, just as happy. He had missed Dummie's ugly mug. And he was also happy that his father hadn't secretly taken him away somewhere, he'd suddenly been very worried about that possibility. Of course, his father wouldn't normally do anything like that, but nothing had been normal since the weekend. Even water from the tap wasn't normal anymore.

"How was school?" Nick asked.

"Fine."

"I mean: did you tell anyone?"

"No, of course not. How were things here?"

"I am Dummie," Dummie said proudly. "I am in the shed."

Angus looked at him in amazement and said, "Blasting cackdingle."

Nick burst out laughing. "I taught him some new words," he said. "And sentences, because words on their own aren't enough. I think he's very clever. He understands almost everything right away. And we did some drawing. You should see what he can do.

He's really very good." He looked over at Dummie and smiled and suddenly Angus felt a stab of jealousy. While he'd been working his guts off at school, his father and Dummie had been having fun!

"I've been good too, because I didn't say anything!" he said angrily.

Nick pinched his cheek. "I know that you are both good boys," he said. "And now it's your turn, Angus, so I can finally get down to work. Will you teach Dummie some new sentences?"

This was something Angus was keen to do, of course! And he shouldn't be so childish. Being jealous of a mummy, wasn't that bonkers? He took Dummie back into the house, got himself a glass of juice and got down to work, teaching Dummie new sentences. He started with: "This is juice." And then, "I drink juice." And that's how it went on. His father had told him just to say all the sentences, and not to talk to Dummie as if he was a baby, because otherwise Dummie would think that baby talk was normal. So he taught Dummie difficult sentences while they played, while he went on the swing and Dummie sat above him in the tree, while he and Nick ate, and while they watched television.

Before they knew it the day was over. Dummie had learned at least a hundred new sentences.

"I am berry ghood," Dummie said as he lay in bed playing with his scarab.

"Not berry ghood but very good," Angus said sternly.

"But that's what I say. I am berry ghood," Dummie said proudly.

The next day they did exactly the same thing. Angus went to school and Dummie spent the day drawing with Nick. After school, Angus taught Dummie words and sentences. They played, fooled around and argued. Dummie didn't eat and fell out of the tree from time to time. Angus already found it difficult to imagine how things were before he came. And he found it even more difficult to imagine what it would be like if Dummie wasn't there anymore. And although his father sometimes screwed up his face into more wrinkles than Mr Scribble had, Angus was sure that he was happy that Dummie was there too.

"Has he told you anything about his old life?" Nick asked one evening, some time during the second week. That was a coincidence, because Angus had had the same thought that very afternoon. Soon Dummie would know enough sentences to be able to tell them about himself.

Angus shook his head.

"Perhaps he's forgotten everything," Nick said. "It might be for the best."

"Why?" Angus asked.

"What we don't know, doesn't hurt us," his father said. "If he can't remember his old life, he won't miss it."

But Dummie hadn't forgotten it completely, as they found out half an hour later. He was sitting with Angus watching television and the programme had just finished. Angus wanted to turn off the television, but Dummie grabbed the remote control and pressed all the buttons. He did that every evening, because he was fascinated by the way each button gave you something different to see.

All of a sudden he began to scream. He stared wide-eyed at an enormous pyramid on the screen. He rushed to the television, pressed his face against the picture and started crying out, "There I live! I live! There! My dad!" And then a lot of incomprehensible words. Angus quickly fetched his father. They looked at Dummie, who was hugging the television and shouting and pointing. Angus and Nick sat down on the sofa and waited until the programme had finished because they didn't know what else to do. They saw deserts and camels and statues and tombs and pyramids.

After a quarter of an hour, the credits appeared. Dummie got hold of the remote and began frantically pressing all the buttons. But the pyramids didn't return. He looked at the back of the television to see whether they might possibly be there. He turned around and pointed at the television. "There I live," he said. "My dad." He suddenly gave the television a hard whack. "SIRSAR!" he cried. Then he ran upstairs.

Angus looked at his father in fright.

"Just go to him," Nick said. "I'll come up in ten minutes."

Angus went upstairs. Dummie was sitting on the bed, his shoulders slumped. He was holding the scarab and stroking its smooth wings. "I am DARWISHI UR-ATUM MSAMAKI MINKABH ISHAQ EBONI," he whispered. "My dad gone. I want my dad." He went over to Angus' desk and picked up a pencil and paper and drew a man on a throne. On his head he drew a crown with a scarab. Angus held his breath. Was this Dummie's father? Was Dummie a pharaoh's son?

"Dad is AᴋHNETUT," Dummie said. He drew a woman with shoulder-length hair and gave Angus a questioning look.

"Mum," Angus said. He hadn't taught Dummie that word because there wasn't a mother in the house.

"Mum is ENISIS," Dummie said with a sigh.

He suddenly began to explain everything. "This is SCARAB OF MUᴋATAGARA. Scarab goes on my dad's ghead. I am sick. GHEPSETSUT gives me

scarab. I get warm. Lots quiet talking. My dad say I
go on journey. Ghe doesn't come, but ꜱ ᴄ ᴀ ʀ ᴀ ʙ ᴏ ꜰ
ᴍ ᴜ ᴋ ᴀ ᴛ ᴀ ɢ ᴀ ʀ ᴀ ghelp me. Understand?"

Angus nods. He understands completely.

And then Dummie asked him a dreadful question.
He asked, "Where is my dad?"

Angus felt hot. Was he supposed to tell Dummie
that his father was dead and probably had been for
more than 4,000 years? And that he'd never see him
again? Did he actually understand that he was in a
different century now?

"Where is dad?!" Dummie cried in a rush of anger.

Angus quickly got up, got out an atlas and looked
for a map of the world. "We are here," he said, pointing
at the Netherlands. "And you used to live there." Then
he pointed at Egypt. "That's a long way from here.
You would have to walk for a thousand days. Or even
longer, I expect."

"When we going to do that?" Dummie asked.

Angus felt even hotter. Did Dummie really think
that his father was still alive? "Your country, on the
television, that's a very long time ago," he said quietly.
"Not yesterday, but a thousand times yesterday. And
then much longer."

Dummie looked at him wide-eyed. "Not possible,"
he said.

"No, it's not possible," Angus whispered. "But it
happened."

Dummie squeezed the scarab so hard that the
bandages around his knuckles almost burst. He turned
around. "I want my mum and dad," he moaned. Then

he sobbed. Then he sobbed again. And then Dummie began to wail. Angus sat down next to him, but Dummie pushed him away. He was crying even more than when they'd found him in Angus' wardrobe. All of a sudden Angus started to cry too and they sat there crying on Dummie's bed together.

I want my mum and dad

Luckily Nick came into the bedroom just then.

"Dummie told me about his mum and dad," Angus sobbed. "I said we can't ever go to them. I want— Dad, do something!"

Nick took Dummie onto his lap and rocked him gently backwards and forwards. After a while Dummie stopped crying.

"Come on, let's go for a drive," Nick said. He stuck

down the flap over Dummie's sad face, took hold of his hand and pulled him downstairs.

Dummie was allowed to sit in the front and Angus had to go in the back. Nick fastened Dummie's seatbelt, started the engine and drew off. They drove through the dark streets. Dummie stared and stared. Nick drove along the motorway, along a riverbank, through the village and past the shops. Angus thought that his father wanted to show Dummie that they weren't in Egypt. That they were living in a different time. That Dummie really was in a totally different place. To be honest, he wasn't really sure what his father wanted, but it did work. After a while, Dummie pressed his face against his window and just looked.

When they finally turned back into the driveway, Dummie let out a deep sigh. Nick turned on the windscreen wipers. He pressed all of the buttons repeatedly until Dummie joined in. After that they couldn't get Dummie out of the car. He flicked the headlights on and off, left the windscreen wipers going and had the car radio blaring out across the garden at full volume. Nick just left the key in the ignition because Dummie had stopped thinking about Egypt, his mother and father and camels for now. The only camel he was thinking about was the car, which he called a "camel with wheels'.

That night, Angus waited until Dummie had fallen asleep. Then he crept out of bed and wrote down the names Dummie had said. Akhnetut. Enisis. Mukatagara. He carefully picked up the green book on

Dummie's bedside table and went downstairs.

"Trouble sleeping again?" Nick asked.

Angus showed him the note. "These are the names Dummie mentioned. The first two are his mother and father. Shall we look them up? And maybe take another look at the hieroglyphics?"

Nick smiled. "Good idea, son," he said. He turned on the computer and they looked up the names together. There was just one Akhnetut listed together with an Enisis, and that was a pharaoh from the sixth dynasty. He had reigned for just two years and very little was known about him. They hadn't even found his grave. There was nothing about a scarab or a son who died young. And Mukatagara was just an old city.

"Maybe this Akhnetut was his father," Nick muttered. "But then we still don't know anything."

He opened the green book and compared it to the pages on the computer with hieroglyphics, but it was just as impossible to make anything of it as the last time. After a while, Nick simply turned off the computer. "Angus, it doesn't matter a bit," he said, like last time. "It's about the here and now. And that keeps us busy enough. Just try to sleep. Night, night."

Angus gave his father a kiss and went back upstairs. His father was right. Even if Dummie was Tutankhamun's brother, it didn't make the slightest bit of difference now.

CHAPTER 4

A Very Bad Idea

One Saturday, Nick wanted to talk to Angus about something.

Dummie had been staying with them for a couple of weeks by then, and his being there had become the most normal thing in the world. Angus went to school, where he didn't say anything about Dummie; and Dummie sat drawing with Nick in the shed. He had practised as much as he could and by now he could speak the language quite well. But more and more often he just sat there staring into the distance. Or he put on the television to see whether his country was inside that funny cupboard again. Or he sat at the window staring outside.

A couple of times, Angus had already thought back to what his father had said about a new kitten having to learn everything. Once a cat has learned the rules, it likes to just lie around in the sun, or be stroked or catch mice. But Dummie didn't like lying around one little bit. And he was probably too brainy to have finished learning everything already.

Angus went to the shed, sat down on a stool and listened patiently to his father.

"Dummie is our guest," Nick began. "We've washed him, we've taught him lots of things that are normal for us and he's started to find them normal now too. He can already speak our language a bit and he understands what we want. And even though he can be pigheaded and short-tempered, he doesn't keep pressing all the buttons anymore."

This wasn't completely true, because Dummie had almost trashed the vacuum cleaner yesterday while he'd tried to suck up dirt in the garden. The vacuum cleaner was still his favourite. But Angus listened patiently and wondered what his father really wanted to say. What was the important thing he wanted to discuss?

Nick looked at him. And then he said it. "Angus, I've thought this through properly," he said, "and I think Dummie should go to school."

"To school?" Angus gaped at his father. Why school? Then everyone would see him! Everyone would ask questions. They would discover his secret. Then they'd come and fetch Dummie and saw him open, his father had warned him about that. "Why?" he asked aghast.

"Because he's bored," Nick said. "He wants to go with you. And all children go to school. I want to talk to Mr Scribble and see whether he can join your class. Dummie knows a lot about Egypt and maybe he can take part in the competition. We'll say he's a burns victim, your second cousin. If we act really normal, no one will think anything of it."

"But everyone will just see that Dummie's a mummy, won't they?" Angus shouted.

"No, because we'll give him new bandages. From the pharmacy's. And if we say he got burned, everyone will just see a burned boy. That's how it works. You see what you think you see."

Angus didn't believe it one little bit, but his father was sure, he said.

"But I wanted to ask you about it first, Angus. You know your class. What do you think?"

Angus looked at his father. His father knew everything, and now he was asking his advice about such a bad idea. He thought it was stupid, of course! Yes, Ebbi would be alright. And most of the boys too. But you couldn't be sure about Annalisa and Lizzy.

"Miss Frick," he said. "She's not very nice."

"Not very nice?" Nick snorted. He had only met her once, when Angus had been punished for something so minor he no longer remembered what it was, but Nick had been so angry and he'd gone to the school and given her a piece of his mind. After that his father had gone on for weeks about "the impossible

arrogance of some people and Miss Frick in particular".
It was a difficult sentence but Angus knew exactly what
he meant – which was that he thought Miss Frick was
a pig.

"But you're right," Nick said. "Dummie would have
to watch out for her. Although he probably wouldn't
see her much."

"Except if he has a tantrum," Angus said. "Then
he'd have to go to her, for punishment."

"Then he'll just have to control himself," Nick said.
"And you'll have to put on a good show. You won't be
able to let anything slip and you'd have to look after
him. Can you manage all that?"

Angus hesitated. Of course he could see that
Dummie was getting bored. But wouldn't it be better to
think of an alternative? He had to go to school to learn
to read and count, and because he wanted to get a good
job when he was older, his father always said. But what
kind of job was Dummie supposed to get later? He'd
never get a job, would he? And Dummie didn't eat, so
he wouldn't grow.

"You can sleep on it," Nick said. "Or discuss it with
Dummie."

Angus nodded. "I'll discuss it with Dummie," he
said reluctantly.

Angus did that right away after lunch.

"I go to school every day, you know," he said.

"I know," Dummie said,
"Do you want to come too?"
Dummie's ugly face began to shine. "Yes!" he shouted at once. "Dummie come too! Nice! I see other children! Nice!"
"But you have to sit still and pay attention too. Even when you don't understand it."
"Nice!" Dummie said.
"And they might think you're weird."
"Nice! Nice!"

He thought everything was nice. Nick was right. Dummie really wanted to go to school.
"Angus and me are friends," Dummie said. "At school friends too?"
Angus began to list the names of other children in his class. "Ebbi. He's cool. And then you've got Bert, Emma, Frank, Anne and lots more. They're all nice. Only Annalisa and Lizzy aren't. They might give you a hard time."

"I'm not scared. I ghave scarab," Dummie said. "Scarab ghelp me."

Angus looked at him. "Dummie, there's something else. If you go to school no one can know who you are."

"I am Dummie," Dummie said.

"Yes, that's right. But not what you look like. Inside. That you're, erm... rotten. You can't let anyone see your face. Really not."

"Yes, I am rotten," Dummie said. "I go tomorrow?"

"No, tomorrow's Sunday. But maybe on Monday."

"Ghooray!" Dummie cried. "I go to school!"

Well. That was clear. Angus went to his father and told him that Dummie really wanted to go to school. "But I'd rather he didn't," he added hesitantly. "I'm afraid he'd give himself away. Or that someone might notice and he'd be taken from us."

Nick squeezed his shoulder. "I'll simply teach him what he can and can't say," he said.

They did this over dinner. Dummie had gone on about school all afternoon. "I go to school," seemed to be the only sentence he could say at the moment. And the word "nice', which he must have said a thousand times.

"Listen carefully, Dummie," Nick began. "You must never, ever say that you are a mummy. Otherwise something terrible will happen." And then he told Dummie about the strange men who might take him away, and if they found out he was a living mummy, they might do horrible things to him. "So never, ever Dummie. Do you understand? Not even once."

"MAASHI," Dummie said. "I am not mummy. Not even once."

"Exactly. You're our relative, a distant nephew of an aunt who moved abroad. You got burned in a fire and now you have bandages. You understand?"

"Yes, I understand," said Dummie.

"Let's practice then," Nick said. "What are you?"

"I am not mummy," said Dummie.

"No, you mustn't say that. You should say, "I got burned.""

"I got burned," Dummie repeated obediently.

Then Nick asked Dummie all the questions the children would also ask him.

"Who are you?"

"I am relative of Angus. I got burned."

"Does it hurt?"

"No."

"Which country are you from?"

"Egypt."

"How old are you?"

"Eight or nine?" Dummie asked. Somehow he didn't know.

"We'll say ten, so that you can be in Angus' class," Nick said.

"I am ten, so I go in Anghus's class," Dummie said.

"Where are your mother and father?"

"I don't know," Dummie said.

"No, you have to say: "They got burned too. They are still in Egypt.""

"They got burned too. They are still in Egypt," Dummie repeated.

This went on for a while. Nick asked questions about his old house and about the fire. About his old school. About his family. They practised all evening until Dummie only gave the right answers.

Nick leaned back in his chair. "I think you're ready," he said.

Angus wasn't sure. "He could just blurt it out," he said.

"He's the cleverest little fellow I ever met," his father said. "He won't blurt anything out."

"Oh," Angus said. It was a shame that he wasn't the cleverest little fellow his father had ever met. But he knew that already really – half of his class were cleverer than he was.

"And one more thing," Nick said to Dummie. "You have to leave your scarab at home."

Dummie shook his head at once.

"I think so," Nick said. "It's a valuable thing, and if anyone steals it, it's gone."

But he could say what he liked, Dummie just said, "No! My scarab!"

Finally Nick gave in. "Then you'll have to keep it well hidden and don't show it to anybody," he said. "And Angus, you're going to spend a day in front of the mirror practising looking innocent."

"I've been practising looking innocent for the past three weeks," Angus said.

"Very good. But with Dummie there too it will be even more difficult. And Dummie, I'll teach you how to ride a bike tomorrow."

Ride a bike? Angus thought. His father thought of everything!

On Sunday, Nick got an old bike of Angus' out of the shed which he'd kept for you-never-know-when-you-might-need-it. He put the saddle down and then it was just right for Dummie.

Dummie was stamping his feet impatiently. He had often seen Angus riding his bike and Angus had even given him a backie once, but they'd fallen off because he was swaying around too much. He didn't want to get on behind Angus anymore after that and had shouted "sɪRsAR!" ten times, which Angus thought meant something like whumpy dumpman or blasting cackdingle.

But getting a bike of his own was different. He kept on shouting, "My bike! My bike!"

Nick helped him get on and held onto the bike. "Pedal and steer," he said.

"I know already," Dummie said.

He began to pedal and Angus and Nick ran along next to the bike. Nick held onto the handlebars.

"Faster! Faster!" Angus cried.

"No, not so fast!" Nick puffed.

"It's good for your fat belly, Dad!" Angus cried. "Come on, Dummie, faster!"

After three circuits, Nick panted that Dummie could do it on his own now. Angus just thought he was tired, but he said that Angus should keep on running next to Dummie.

Dummie began to pedal again. He wobbled along the garden path. His handlebars went all over the place but he didn't fall. "I am good!" he cried.

"MAASHI!" Angus called out. "Go faster then!"

He shouldn't have said that. Dummie suddenly started pedalling three times as fast and only went and rode off the drive and onto the street outside.

"Hey!" Nick roared. "Stop! Brake!"

"You haven't taught him that yet!" Angus cried.

"Whumpy dumpman! Angus, go after him!"

Angus leapt onto his bike and raced after Dummie. "DUMMIE! STOP! COME BACK!" he yelled.

Dummie looked back, screamed with pleasure and pedalled even harder. He was shouting as he went along, a length of bandage streaming behind him. Angus had to cycle like mad to catch up with him. He didn't manage until they had reached the village.

"I'm ghood!" Dummie called out.

"Yes! But you're going the wrong way! Everyone can see you!" Angus cried. "Stop! Don't pedal!"

Dummie stuck both of his legs out sideways.

"No, keep them on the pedals. Pedal backwards! Push back!"

Dummie didn't understand at all. His legs flailing, he wobbled even more. Angus looked around in despair. Still no one to be seen. But that could change at any moment. They reached a crossroads and Dummie turned right. Wrong, Angus thought at once. Just around the corner a woman with peculiar, wide hips was walking along the pavement. Angus only knew one woman with hips like that and that was Miss Frick. Miss Frick was walking along the pavement.

"Just stop now!" Angus cried in terror. "Steer! Turn around! Waaah!"

And then Dummie ran over Miss Frick. He rammed right into her fat bottom and Miss Frick slammed forwards onto her nose with a scream. In a split second, Angus saw her glasses flying through the air. That was really lucky, because the glasses were as thick as the bottom of jam jars and without them she probably couldn't see a thing.

Dummie didn't fall off, and that was the second lucky thing. He just cycled over her, as if his green bike was a mountain bike and Miss Frick a large bump in the landscape.

"Keep on going!" Angus cried as he looked around. Miss Frick scrambled to her feet, ranting and raging. At his wit's end, Angus gave Dummie a shove, causing him to turn right again. They carried on a bit more, Angus pushing and pulling and giving directions until they were finally going the right way again. They lurched back up the driveway at last.

Nick was waiting for them with a worried expression. Dummie still couldn't brake, so Nick stood in front of him and they tumbled onto the grass together.

"I can cycle!" Dummie cried happily.

Nick laughed in relief, until Angus told him that Dummie had knocked down Miss Frick and then ran her over.

"Did she see you?" he asked in horror.

"No, her glasses fell off," Angus said. And he explained that she was still looking for them when they disappeared round the corner.

"That's lucky," Nick said. Suddenly his eyes began to gleam. "You mean, you actually ran her over?" he asked.

"Yes. Right over her bottom," Angus giggled. "And he didn't even fall off his bike."

"Well, that's pretty impressive," Nick said dryly. They both fell about laughing. Dummie didn't get it at all, but laughed along just as heartily.

When they'd stopped laughing, they practised until Dummie could brake. Dummie thought it fantastic. "I'm the boss of the bike!" he cried proudly. "I say bike stop, ghe do it!"

"Tell him he has to go in the shed now," Nick chuckled.

"No. Ghe doesn't want to!" Dummie cried. And he raced around the yard yet another time.

That evening they ate pizza that Nick had made himself. Nick was very good at making pizza, with homemade dough and broccoli, but he only did it if they had something to celebrate.

"Today we're celebrating Dummie going to school," he said.

"Have you already checked whether it's alright?" Angus asked with his mouth full.

"I'll go see Mr Scribble tomorrow and he'll sort it out," Nick said.

He was probably right about that, Angus thought. If there was anyone who wanted the best for everyone, it was Mr Scribble. Apart from his father, that was; his father was the best person in the whole world.

On Monday morning, Angus went to school alone. His father was going to come in at three in the afternoon to talk to Mr Scribble about Dummie.

All day Angus was so worried that he dropped everything and didn't answer a single question correctly. Mr Scribble gave him an astonished look a few times and Angus just smiled shyly back. To make matters worse, Mr Scribble began talking about mummies again in the afternoon. He had dredged up an old book about Egypt from somewhere with beautiful pictures of mummies, and wanted to show them. He talked about balsams and different kinds of linen and he got so carried away that he kept on talking until the bell went.

Finally they all stood up and went outside. Shortly afterwards, Nick went into the classroom.

Mr Scribble didn't even look surprised, he must have thought that Angus' father was coming to explain why his son had been such a scatterbrain all day. He stacked up some exercise books and sat down.

"Good afternoon, Mr Gust," he said in a friendly voice. "So, tell me. What's the matter with Angus?"

"Nothing's the matter with Angus," Nick said. "I'm here about something else." And then he began to lie. Nick Gust, who always said you should be truthful, lied three times in a row.

"Mr Scribble," he began. "We have had to take in a distant relative. A child. His name is Dummie. His parents were seriously injured in a fire and he is staying with us for the time being. He might even stay for much longer. We thought it would be a good idea if he could go to school as usual."

Angus looked at his father's face. Nick had probably practised in front of the mirror because he didn't move a muscle. He looked like he was saying "lovely weather" or something of the sort. Mr Scribble began to ask questions and Nick carried on lying unflappably. Dummie's parents weren't just relatives but also his best friends. Dummie had already stayed with us in the past. And Dummie was so clever he'd skipped a class in Egypt.

"Egypt? He's from Egypt?" Mr Scribble asked in amazement.

"Oh, hadn't I told you that?" Nick said, playing the innocent.

"No. Well that's interesting."

"And a long way from here," Nick joked.

"You could say so. Why didn't he stay there then?"

"Because he couldn't. We're his only family," Nick said.

Mr Scribble rubbed his chin pensively. "This is quite something," he said.

"Sure. And there's another thing," Nick said. "Just a minor matter. Our Dummie is quite bandaged up. He has burns and scars. There are areas which still have to heal. They don't look good. Festering ulcers, the skin's hanging off."

"On his arms or on his legs?" Mr Scribble asked in shock.

"Everywhere. From head to toe."

"From head to toe? On his face too?"

"It was a serious fire," Nick said in a sad voice. "He had to lie in a disinfectant bath for weeks. When he was finally allowed out he was bandaged up. The doctor said there's no way he can take them off. Terrible, isn't it? It itches horribly, sometimes. But anyway. If you want, I can get hold of his old school reports. Papers. Whatever you want. As long as he can come." He even pulled a sorrowful face.

Angus sat there gaping at his father. He thought his tongue was about to drop off. What a good liar his father was! He could be an actor!

There was a short pause.

"Don't worry about his papers," Mr Scribble said then. "But I'll have to discuss it with Miss Frick, she's the boss. I'll do that right away and then I'll call you tomorrow. Give him my best wishes. What was his name again? Dummie you said?"

"Yes," Nick said. "It rhymes with mummy."

Angus couldn't believe his ears. Did his father say mummy? Mr Scribble let them out and Angus was beside himself. "What did you go and say mummy for? And he doesn't have any papers!"

"I was bluffing, son," Nick said. "And all those lies are for the greater good."

"And I've lost my bike key," Angus said dejectedly. This was a lie for the greater good too, the key was in his pocket, but he wanted to try and eavesdrop on Mr Scribble and Miss Frick. "I'll go back and look for it. Why don't you go home to Dummie? I'll be back soon."

As soon as his father was out of sight, Nick walked around the school until he was standing under Miss Frick's window. He was lucky, it was open a chink and Miss Frick's voice echoed through it as though she was speaking into a microphone. Angus pushed the window slightly further open and listened. By the sound of it, Miss Frick was in a terrible mood.

"The answer is no. A boy like that from god-knows-where just takes up too much time and energy," she snapped.

"He's not from god-knows-where, he's from Egypt."

"So what? We're not a refugee camp."

"He's a child!" Mr Scribble said. "What's more,

he's been through hell. He's been burned and is all bandaged up."

"So what? We're not a hospital. We're a school for normal children from Polderdam. And are you sure he doesn't have anything else? Something infectious? Before you know it the whole school will come down with it."

"Why would they lie about that?" Mr Scribble asked.

"Because people can't be trusted," Miss Frick snorted. "I'm responsible for these children's health, and you want me to let in someone wrapped in bandages from head to toe, who might be ill and infectious, and doesn't speak the language."

"That's right," Mr Scribble said.

"And what will the other children think?"

"They'll think: great, a new boy at school."

"We've got enough boys."

It was quiet for a while. Then Mr Scribble started again, and now his voice was all toadyish. "My dear Leonora," he said. "You've run this place for ten years. But I've been at the school longer than anyone else. I know exactly what everyone wants and thinks. And everyone wants us to win the schools' competition. And that's about Egypt. Egypt! Which is where this boy comes from. He can help. And if our school wins, we'll be in the paper. Then everyone will read that the children from Hobble Primary are the cleverest in the region this year. That's good publicity. And what do you think the mayor will say when his daughter's class wins the schools' competition?"

Angus grinned. That was a clever thing to say to, erm... Leonora. He grinned even more. Who on earth had a name like Leonora?

"Your job is to consider how to get the best out of the school," Mr Scribble continued. "Results. That's what it's about. And we'll get them with Dummie."

There was another silence. Miss Frick was clearly thinking it over. Maybe she liked toadying and was going to fall for it.

Angus stood there listening and was so tense that he suddenly got a cramp. He shot up and hit his head against the window.

"What was that?" Miss Frick said. There were

footsteps. Angus dived behind a bush and crouched there very still, which was difficult because the cramp was really hurting. He saw Miss Frick's head peering out of the window and looking left and right. There was a plaster on her nose and a large scratch on her cheek. What an ugly face she had, he thought. He'd rather look at Dummie. The window slammed shut.

Angus waited for at least five minutes before running to his bike and sprinting home. Miss Frick didn't want Dummie to come to school. Angus didn't know whether to feel relieved or disappointed.

Nick was sitting with Dummie next to the telephone in the sitting room and waiting.

"I don't think he's allowed," Angus said as he walked in.

"What do you mean?"

Angus told them that he'd been listening in and that Miss Frick was worried that the boy from god-knows-where had an infectious disease.

"What nonsense. He's just burned," his father said.

"He's not. He's a mummy," Angus said. "And Mr Scribble said that he could help with the competition. But Miss Frick said that she was the boss."

The phone rang. Nick picked up, listened, nodded and said, "We'll be there at half-past nine tomorrow then. Thank you."

He hung up with a broad smile. "It worked," he chuckled. "Dummie, my lad, you're going to school."

And Angus thought: blasting cackdingle.

That evening they wrapped Dummie in fresh bandages. Wrapping him up again was quite a job. Nick had bought three large rolls on Saturday, apparently, and gave one to Angus. Angus was supposed to walk around Dummie with the roll and his father would make sure that everything ended up in the right place.

"Not too tight!" Nick said.

"But not too loose either, otherwise it'll fall off," said Angus. He'd run ten rings around Dummie and had at least a hundred to go. "Why don't you turn too, then it'll go faster," he whispered to Dummie.

Dummie put his arms in the air and began to spin. He smiled and went faster. And faster. "MAASHI! MAASHI!" he cried.

"Ho! Not so fast! Wait a minute!" Nick cried.

"MAAAAAASHI!" Dummie pirouetted, lost his balance and bumped into the table. He fell, grabbed at the first thing to hand and pulled the table cloth, fruit bowl and contents over himself.

"Waaah! I see dark!" he screamed.

"Whumpy dumpman," Nick muttered. "You're a wild one."

Angus got the giggles so badly his stomach hurt. He carried on hiccupping and they had to wait ages before they could start again. "Dummie, stand still! And Angus, walk!" Nick said sternly.

At last they'd finished. Dummie looked sparkling white. He went over to the mirror curiously. "Lovely. Nice!" he said. He still found everything nice. Just as long as he could go to school.

Then it was bedtime.

Neither Dummie nor Angus could get to sleep. Dummie was too excited and Angus was too nervous. This whole school business was not a good idea. If something went wrong tomorrow, the whole world would find out that that there was a living mummy in Polderdam. Something like that would be on the news in every country. And then they'd take Dummie away from them.

"You mustn't stand out too much," he explained to Dummie again. "You have to sit nicely in your chair, just listen and do your best. And you mustn't get into any arguments, otherwise you'll have to go to Miss Frick."

"I not afraid of Miss Frick."

"But you'll have to be nice to her."

"Yes, I understand, Angus," Dummie said.

Yes, yes, Angus thought. All of a sudden he had an idea. He got out of bed, get a piece of paper and drew a face with long, straight hair. He drew dark eyebrows, glasses and an angry mouth, drooping down on both sides.

Dummie stuck out his tongue. "That is ugly face," he shuddered.

"Wait until she turns up her nose, then she looks like a pig," Angus chuckled. He cut out the face, attached a rubber band to it and put it around his head.

"Pay attention, we're going to practise. I am Miss Frick and you are Dummie. I will be horrible and you will be nice."

"MAASHI. I be nice. Ghello, Miss Frick," Dummie said.

Angus put on a nasty voice. "Go away, you burned Egyptian boy."

"You go away," Dummie replied at once.

"Wrong!" Angus said. "You can't say that. You have to just turn around and walk away."

"Why?"

"Because she's the boss!" He imitated Miss Frick's voice again and said, "Dummie, I find you disgusting. You are a danger to the children of Polderdam. I think you are a dirty, ugly, stinking..."

Dummie took a swing and punched the mask.

Angus stumbled backwards, shocked. "Ouch!" he cried. "What are you doing?"

"I ghit ugly person," Dummie said angrily.

"But it's me!" Angus said.

"No. You are Miss Frick!"

Angus took off the mask and rubbed his forehead. "Have you gone mad? You can't hit people!"

"She act ugly," Dummie said stubbornly.

"But you can't!" said Angus. He screwed Miss Frick's face into a ball and threw it in the bin. Well, that was a disaster. Dummie was too much of a hothead. But he had made Miss Frick say really nasty things. The real Miss Frick wouldn't say things like that. "There are two girls you have to watch out for too," he said. "One is called Annalisa and the other Lizzy. Annalisa Stickler is the worst. She's the mayor's daughter."

"What is mayor?"

"That's the boss of the city. A kind of pharaoh. Well, a small one," Angus explained. "Annalisa is mean.

Inside she's maybe even more rotten than you. Really stupid. And Lizzy is her stupid friend."

"I not afraid of girls," Dummie said.

"You don't need to be," Angus said. "And they might not do anything. But if they do, you have to watch out. You're not allowed to hit them, in any case."

They lay back down in bed. Dummie got out his scarab and turned it around. Angus looked at the golden object. "Why do you absolutely have to take that with you?" he asked.

Dummie didn't hesitate. "Because I can't be without scarab," he said. "Without scarab I am dead."

Angus thought of the drawing Dummie had made, when he'd just arrived, with the lightning strike right onto the scarab. That's why he had woken up, he and his father thought. No wonder the scarab was so important to him.

CHAPTER 5

Off to School

The next morning they got up early. Nick prepared two rucksacks. In Dummie's he put a can of air freshener in case he began to smell, and an empty lunchbox and a beaker. "Just like everyone else, then he won't stand out," he said. As though a mummy with a bag wouldn't stand out as much as a mummy without one, thought Angus.

Dummie had to wear Angus' old clothes and a pair of trainers. "Ghappy to gho, nice! See you later!" he said happily.

Angus got on his bike. "See you later!" he called out, as cheerfully as he could.

"Yes, nice! Nice!" Dummie cried.

Angus cycled slowly to school. Nice? Nice? He suddenly had a terrible ache in his stomach, that's how nice it was. The closer he got to the school, the more sure he became. Everyone would see at once that Dummie was a mummy. Did his father really think that anyone would fall for it? They'd take him away that very afternoon and stick pins in him. He wouldn't feel that but afterwards they'd saw open his skull and even a dead mummy wouldn't be able to survive that.

By the time Angus got to school, he was stiff with nerves. His fingers were shaking so much he couldn't lock his bike. Maybe he was suffering from shock too. He walked into the classroom with leaden feet.

Mr Scribble had put an extra table next to his. He looked up and winked at Angus. When everyone had arrived he stood up in front of the class and winked at Angus a second time. "Girls and boys, I have some good news. We're welcoming a new boy in the class," he said.

There was a short silence.

"Is he good-looking?" Annalisa asked.

A few girls giggled.

"I want to talk to you about that. This boy has been in a terrible accident and got badly burned. That's why he's bandaged up. He is living with Angus for a while, because his parents can't look after him. He is from another country and doesn't speak our language that well yet. He's from Egypt."

"Burned?"

"From Egypt?"

"At Angus'?"

"Is that his table?"

Mr Scribble smiled. "And do you know what the best thing is?" he asked.

"The schools' competition," Ebbi said cleverly. "He can help us."

"Exactly," Mr Scribble said.

"Has he got scars from the burns?" someone asked.

"I think so," Mr Scribble said. "But you won't see them. They're under his bandages."

"What about his face? Has he got scars on his face too?"

"His face is bandaged up too."

"His face too?" There was a loud din.

So far it sounds alright, Angus thought. He was just breathing out in relief when Annalisa made a joke: "So we're getting a mummy in the class?" Angus felt a new stab of pain in his stomach. Mummy. There it was. Anyone wearing bandages was a mummy.

"That kind of joke isn't pleasant!" Mr Scribble warned. "I want all of you to be nice to him. You too."

Annalisa shrugged. "He'll have to be nice first. And

if you can't even see his face... Maybe he'll be laughing at us behind our backs."

"Why would he do that?" Ebbi purred. "You don't have a spotty nose, do you? Oh, perhaps you do."

A few children laughed. Annalisa gave Ebbi a bad-tempered look. She did have a spot on her nose today, Angus noticed.

"Where is he then?" Ebbi asked.

"He will be here at half-past nine," Mr Scribble said. "We'll do some maths until then."

So they had a maths lesson. Everyone waited excitedly for half past nine. The children spent more time looking out of the window than at their exercise books. Angus too. He made a half-hearted attempt but sums were the last thing on his mind. He mustn't say the wrong thing. Dummie mustn't say the wrong thing.

Was the Velcro stitched on well enough? What if someone picked at Dummie's bandages and saw the real ones underneath?

All of a sudden, someone said, "There he is!" They all rushed over to the window.

Nick cycled into the playground with Dummie. Dummie was wearing one of Angus' old coats and on his back he had the rucksack with the empty lunchbox, beaker and air freshener. They stowed their bikes in the rack and walked to the door.

The class went quiet. No one looked out of the window anymore, but at the door.

Not long afterwards there was a knock, and then it became even more quiet.

Mr Scribble opened the door and there were Nick and Dummie. Dummie had the flap in front of his face and a red cap on.

"Oh," someone cried out in shock.

"What a lot of bandages," Ebbi whispered.

Angus' heart beat like a drum. How did his father manage to stand there so calmly? It was as clear as day, wasn't it? There was a mummy wearing a cap in the classroom. Anyone who couldn't see it needed a pair of glasses like Miss Frick's. Angus waited anxiously for someone to scream. In his mind he pictured men with saws. No, chainsaws!

"Girls and boys, this is Dummie," Mr Scribble said solemnly.

No one began to scream, because everyone had gone mad. No one saw a mummy, they all saw a boy with burns.

You see what you think you are seeing, Nick had said. Did it really work like that? Did Angus only see a mummy because he knew that Dummie was one?

"SABA EL CHIR," Mr Scribble said. "That means good morning."

"SABA EL CHIR," a few children repeated.

"Ghallo," Dummie said.

Annalisa burst out laughing, and Mr Scribble gave her a warning look.

"Well, have fun, kid," Nick said. He made the thumbs up sign, winked at Angus and left. Great, Angus thought. Great. Lots of grown ups winking at me.

Dummie sat down in the empty seat next to Angus. He was given his own exercise book and a pen, and that was all. Nothing else really happened. Well, everyone stared at Dummie, but Angus had done that too at first. And there were a few whispers. Angus had done that too. But while Angus sat there waiting for them to come to their senses, the others just got on with their sums. Dummie didn't. He was staring at the posters of Egypt. Angus couldn't see his face but those golden eyes were surely wide open in amazement. It was quite a while before Dummie turned to the sums on the board. He copied them down and then began to sketch Mr Scribble. From time to time he turned in his chair and waved at a few children. There were sniggers. Angus was sure Mr Scribble saw everything, but didn't intervene.

It was break time before Angus knew it. He went outside with Dummie and the whole class immediately surrounded them.

"Does it hurt?" someone asked.

"No," Angus replied before Dummie could speak.

"Can you touch it?"

"Better not," Angus said.

Others asked about Egypt and the fire. Angus answered them off the top of his head, but he didn't really need to because they were all talking at once. Dummie nodded a few times. Angus thought he was enjoying it. He hated it himself. It was at least ten minutes before the break ended. Dummie could make at least ten mistakes in ten minutes. Or even a hundred.

All of a sudden Angus got the feeling that somebody was watching them. He turned around and saw Miss Frick by the door. She didn't say anything, she just stood there staring at Dummie. Angus quickly looked the other way. Did she see it then? Someone must see it.

"Shall we play soccer?" Ebbi asked. He fetched a ball and they used their coats to make two goals.

To everyone's surprise, Dummie was better at soccer than anyone else in the playground. He was as quick as lightning, overtook even the fastest boys and scored three times in a row. Everyone cheered. That wasn't what they had expected from a poor, burned boy. And Angus hadn't expected it from a mummy! Almost automatically his head filled up with worries again – that Dummie's bandages would come loose, and that everyone would see his nasty brown, er... legs. Or that one of them might accidentally kick a hole in him. Or that his head would roll off if he headed the ball. Angus imagined worse and worse things and got more and more scared. But nothing at all happened. When they went back into the classroom panting ten minutes later, all of Dummie's bandages were still in place and his head was still on his shoulders. Angus could have kicked himself. He shouldn't get so worked up. It was all going well!

Dummie was given a cautious pat on the shoulder and then another.

"You're good, man!" Ebbi called out. "You can join the soccer team. As striker."

"Yes, I am ghood," Dummie repeated, laughing.

After the break they had a lesson about Egypt. Mr Scribble began to explain about different kinds of graves. He showed them pictures and Dummie was allowed to say what he saw. Luckily Dummie didn't say anything like: "That's the kind of grave I was in!" or "I used to play with that pharaoh!" He just gave simple answers. Sometimes he didn't know the Dutch words but then Mr Scribble would just say, "all in good time", and wink yet again. He didn't have the faintest suspicion. Neither did anyone else. Dummie was just a boy with burns from Egypt, who didn't speak the language very well, but who was good at football. It was unbelievable, yet it did seem that a living mummy could just go to school.

The bell went at midday. Angus and Dummie left the classroom and all of a sudden someone said, "You stink."

Angus turned round with a jolt. Annalisa was

standing behind them. Angus quickly sniffed for a smell of rotting eggs but there was only air freshener. "Leave it out," he said.

Annalisa gave Dummie a mocking look. "It's true, though. He smells like horrid perfume."

"And you smell like Annalisa," Angus said.

Dummie looked from Angus to Annalisa. "You are Annalisa? Shut up or I be angry."

Annalisa looked at Dummie in surprise. "Shut up yourself, you walking first aid kit." She turned on her heels and walked off. Angus quickly pulled Dummie in the opposite direction.

During the lunch break, the children at Hobble's always stayed at school and ate in the assembly hall. Since Dummie didn't eat, he had to pretend. While everyone around him emptied their lunchboxes, he opened his beaker, lifted up his flap and pretended to drink. He was very quick and to Angus' relief, no one saw his face. Ebbi wanted to play football again after they'd eaten and before long the bell went again. The class went inside in good spirits.

Mr Scribble wasn't there yet and Ebbi picked up a pen. "Can I write my name on your arm?" he asked Dummie.

"Why?" Dummie asked.

"It's what you always do on a cast?"

"Cars?"

"That's hard bandage. Come on, here." Ebbi pushed up Dummie's sleeve and wrote EBBI on the bandages in large red letters. Dummie didn't understand a thing but he liked what he saw. "MAASHI! MAASHI!" he cried.

"What's MAASHI?" Ebbi chuckled.

"MAASHI is good! OK!"

"OK. MAASHI!" Ebbi cried.

Then they all wanted to write their names on his cast. They had to form a queue. There were twenty-four children in the class but Dummie had enough bandages. "MAASHI! MAASHI!" he cried every time a new name was added.

"MAASHI!" the others cried back.

Angus tried not to think about the nibs of the pens. Surely they couldn't prick through Dummie's bandages, could they? And Dummie wouldn't leak, would he? Or would he? Stop it! He hissed to himself.

Annalisa was at the back of the queue. She was probably only standing there because Dummie was so popular with the other children. She was holding a green pen and removed the lid.

"Not you," Dummie said.

Annalisa froze.

"You are first-aid kit," Dummie said. "Angus say you stupid. So I say too you stupid. You not write."

A few children tittered, but Angus didn't. Annalisa was more stupid than three ambulances full of first-aid kits, but it was even more stupid to pick a row with her.

Annalisa became furious. Her eyes narrowed and she looked at Dummie as though he was some kind of nasty little creature.

"Huh. I didn't even want to write on your arm," she said haughtily.

"Did," Dummie said. "You have pencil. But you can't. Gho away." This time some children laughed out loud. Annalisa opened her mouth, but luckily Mr Scribble came in at that moment. He saw Dummie's arm with all the names on it, picked up a felt-tip and wrote: Marius Scribble. Mr Scribble had never told them his first name and now everyone shouted, "MAASHI! MAASHI!" Angus sighed with relief: the children in his class all really liked Dummie.

Dummie impressed them most of all with his antics during the afternoon break. It was actually an accident because he fell off the climbing frame. He climbed more quickly than anyone else and one time he even hung upside down. And then he fell, from the top bar. They all saw him fall because they all wanted to be around him all the time. He fell nastily, head first and with a dull thud. There was a sudden silence. Dummie sat there dazed for a while and then got up, shook his head and climbed back up again. "Nice! Nice!" he cried when he had got to the top again.

"He's a tough guy," Angus heard someone say.

"Unbelievable," someone else said.

Stupid, Angus thought. He made a mental note to tell Dummie after school that he should at least pretend that it hurt if he broke his neck. He took a discreet look around. Only Annalisa was looking at Dummie with a nasty expression. But she was probably too cross to think clearly.

And so they reached three o'clock without Dummie becoming a mummy.

Mr Scribble said, "ME-HA SALAMA."

Dummie didn't reply.

"ME-HA SALAMA," Mr Scribble repeated.

"I don't understand," Dummie said.

"Then perhaps I'm not pronouncing it properly," Mr Scribble laughed. "How do you say "Goodbye, see you soon"? He waved in demonstration.

"GHRAH SHAALI," Dummie said,

Mr Scribble shrugged in amazement. "Never heard that," he said. "Must be a dialect. Well, GRAH SHAALI."

"See you soon," Dummie said.

Angus and Dummie fetched their bikes and a few children called out, "Bye Dummie, see you tomorrow!"

And that was the end of Dummie's first day at school. Angus was so relieved. He sighed so deeply the sigh practically came out of his toenails.

"Hey, there's that dumb stink-bag," came Annalisa's voice. She and Lizzy caught up with them. "A boy who smells of perfume is a wuss. Wuss! Wuss! Or are you secretly a girl under all those bandages?"

"Don't say anything," Angus hissed. The girls turned right and the boys left.

"What is wuss?" Dummie asked.

"That's a swearword. They're calling you stupid."

"Stupid is same as wuss?"

"Or thick-head. Or just stupid."

"OK," Dummie said. "Then I say it back tomorrow."

"No. Don't. You mustn't get into a fight," Angus warned.

"They want fight. But I am stronger," Dummie said.

"That's only alright if you get into a fight with a boy. If you get into a fight with a girl you have to be clever."

"I am clever. School is nice! Nice!" He swerved happily towards Angus, who almost bumped into the curb.

As they cycled up to the house, they saw Nick waiting for them on the bench outside. "How was it?" he asked expectantly.

Dummie proudly showed him his arm with all the names on it. "I am good," he said.

"Yes. But it was terrible too," Angus sighed.

"What do you mean?" his father asked in concern.

Angus told him that everything had gone well and that no one had suspected anything, not even when

Dummie fell off the climbing frame. That they actually all thought he was really cool because he was so good at football and because he'd put Annalisa in her place. "Everything went really well, but I was so nervous the whole time. I'm really tired," he said.

Nick wrapped his arm around Angus. "Sounds like it's harder for you than it is for him," he said. "Hang in there, Angus. You need to believe it's possible. And that it's going to work out. You're not normally so anxious."

"But this isn't normal!" Angus said.

"It's not normal, but it is nice, isn't it? Why don't you go and kick a ball around. Give that ball a really hard kick. That helps."

Dummie got the ball out of the shed and kicked it to Angus. Angus kicked it back a few times really hard. His father was right, it did help him let off steam.

"You are good at football," Nick smiled at Dummie. "Did you used to play then?"

"We did with ball. Or with ghead," Dummie said. "Of enemy. Dead ghead."

"What?!" Angus stopped, aghast.

Nick chuckled. "Yes, I once read that somewhere. Children used to play football with the skulls of dead enemies, because sometimes they didn't have a ball."

Angus stared at Dummie in disbelief. "I wouldn't use your head as a football," he cried.

"I am not enemy. And I am not dead," Dummie said. And then he kicked the ball really hard between the ropes of the swing.

Angus shook his head. Dummie wasn't an enemy,

that was true. But he was dead. Or at least he had been. It wouldn't take much more to drive you mad.

They ate broccoli soup, played a game and watched television.

Everything had gone well, Angus thought that evening in bed. He had to believe in it, his father had said. MAASHI, he would.

The next morning Angus cycled to school in better spirits. He had slept well and had given Dummie a fright in the morning by wrapping bandages around his own head and shaking him awake, mooing like a cow. Dummie had screamed his head off and his father had rushed into the bedroom so fast he'd tripped and landed on top of Dummie. Dummie had immediately given him a punch on his nose and then they'd all rolled around until they'd fallen through Angus' bed. All three of them had had a fit of giggles. Angus chuckled to himself as he thought of his father at home mending the bed with a red nose. Dummie was eager to get to school and he was too. Who cared about Annalisa and her childish nonsense? He would just ignore her.

But within five minutes his happy mood had vanished.

"Look, there's that dumbo stink-bag," Annalisa called as Angus and Dummie cycled onto the playground. "Stink-bag! Stink-bag!"

"You are wuss!" Dummie shouted back. "You are thick-ghead! Stupid! Stupid! Stupid!"

Annalisa pinched her nose. "I don't talk to no-face, dumb-dummy stink-bags," she said haughtily.

Angus saw Dummie drawing his hand into a fist and quickly pulled him off in the other direction. "Just leave it," he said.

A little while later Annalisa pinched her nose again in the classroom and screwed up her face very noticeably. "Can I open a window! It stinks here," she complained.

"Don't be a moron," Ebbi said. He knew what she was getting at. Most of the other children did too, actually. And they weren't planning on joining in.

Annalisa carried on moaning about a bad smell in the classroom all morning, and the others played with Dummie in the break as though he smelled of freshly-baked cake. They ignored Annalisa. This would only make her even nastier, Angus thought.

Dummie did his best all morning. Mr Scribble gave him a maths book and he sat there obediently, puzzling away at it.

When the bell went for lunch, Mr Scribble asked Dummie to stay back for a minute. Angus stayed behind too.

"Is everything going well?" Mr Scribble asked in a friendly voice, when the other children had left.

"Very good," Dummie said cheerfully.

Then Mr Scribble told Dummie about the schools' competition. He asked Dummie whether he wanted to join in, since he knew so much about Egypt. Dummie didn't have a clue what a schools" competition was but he said he thought it was nice. Of course. Everything was nice to Dummie.

"Which part of Egypt are you actually from?" Mr Scribble asked with interest.

Angus pricked up his ears.

"Next to Nile," said Dummie.

"And what's the name of your town?"

"Town called Ghishei," Dummie said,

"Do you mean Gizeh?" Mr Scribble asked. "Child! Then you're blessed! If I want to see the pyramids, I have to go on holiday!"

"Me too. But not all finished," Dummie said.

Mr Scribble gave him a confused look but Angus

knew exactly what Dummie meant. "Erm... shall we go and eat? Then we can play football afterwards," he said hurriedly. "Dummie loves football."

"Oh. Yes, of course. Hurry along. We'll talk about it later," Mr Scribble smiled.

Well, not if it was up to Angus! Mr Scribble wasn't stupid. There were more things Dummie could trip up on than his father thought. They'd have to talk about that at home.

They went into the corridor and picked up their bags. "Bag open," Dummie exclaimed.

Angus tensed. He knew that the zip had been closed this morning. He quickly looked in the bag. Dummie's lunchbox and beaker were still there but the air freshener had gone. "Someone's been messing around with your stuff," he said. He bent down and scanned the floor underneath the coats. When he got up again, he found himself staring Annalisa in the face. She had the can in her hand and was screwing up her face. "Lost something?" she taunted Dummie.

"Give ghere," Dummie said angrily. "Is mine."

"What's it for? Is it for your nasty smell? Oh no, of course, it's Egyptian perfume! Catch it if you can! Here Lizzy, catch." She threw the can in an arch towards Lizzy, who was standing a short way off.

Dummie lost his temper. He stormed up to Lizzy and before Angus could stop him he had grabbed the can, turned it on Annalisa and sprayed it all over her. Annalisa began to scream blue murder. Her eyes began to water, she coughed and spat on the ground a few times. "Stupid little pig! You'll be sorry!" she

screamed, half crying. "You... you...!" Then she ran into the toilets.

Angus was completely shocked. "How could you do something like that?" he shouted.

"Because she is stupid wuss," Dummy said angrily. "If she do again, I ghit her ghead."

"No!"

"Yes!" Dummie said. He really meant it and Angus shuddered. Anyone who had footballed with their enemy's head probably wouldn't think twice about giving someone a nosebleed.

They went into the assembly hall to eat. Angus had almost finished when Annalisa came in with her bag. She sat down in the opposite corner and didn't say a word. Her eyes were red, but furious. It wasn't over yet.

After the lunch break, Mr Scribble called Dummie up
to the front.

"Dummie is from Gizeh," he said to the children.
"I think we are all curious about that. So Dummie, can
you tell us something about the pyramids?"

Angus flushed. Now Dummie would really have to
watch what he said. He'd understand that, wouldn't
he?

"Pyramids is big," Dummie said. "Big stones. Lots
of work. They do with wood. Is lots of work. Many
accidents with stones. My family don't work there. Not
for pharaohs."

Wrong, Angus through. He felt even warmer.

"Have you ever been inside one?" Ebbi asked.

"No. Not allowed," Dummie said. "Is for pharaoh.

But I can climb up. Until finished. Then not. I have no pyramid. I am not pharaoh. I am burned boy from Egypt."

It was too much for Angus and he caught his breath. But Mr Scribble laughed. "For someone who hasn't been here that long, you can say quite a lot," he said. "And you know the good news, kids? Dummie wants to join in with the schools' competition. We'll just have to help him learn the language really fast! Sit down, Dummie."

Dummie sank into his chair and Angus breathed out again. That was close. He turned around and looked at Annalisa. She still had red eyes, but she didn't say anything, or pinch her nose.

In the break they played football again and at three o'clock they fetched their bikes.

Dummie got onto his bike, rode a few metres and then got off again. "Bike not good. Broken?" he asked.

Angus checked out Dummie's bike. "No, you've got a flat tyre," he said. He fetched a pump from the school building and turned the lid on the valve.

"What is that?" Dummie asked curiously.

"This is a pump," Angus said. "It makes wind. Watch." He held the tube up to Dummie's face and pumped.

Dummie almost jumped out of his skin and almost knocked the pump out of Angus' hands.

"Stop it, you hothead!" Angus cried out. Grinning, he pumped up Dummie's tyre. But the tyre went down again immediately. "I think it's punctured," Angus said in disappointment. "That's all we need." He got up again, turned around and bumped into Annalisa.

"Got a flat tyre, have you? Then you'll have to walk, stink-bag," Annalisa said. She laughed, stuck her arm through Lizzy's and walked away.

Angus looked from them to the flat tyre and back again. As he returned the pump he kept picturing their two-faced smiles. Could the two girls have pricked a hole in the tyre? He was sure of it. Pff, he'd better not tell Dummie.

They pushed their bikes home. Nick was waiting in the garden.

"Dummie had a flat tyre," Angus said. And then he went on to say that Dummie had covered Annalisa with air freshener. "Dad, you have to tell him it's not allowed. Annalisa is really annoying, but Dummie just gets too angry. He wants to hit her. And Mr Scribble asked Dummie which part of Egypt he came from. And then he had to tell us about pyramids this afternoon. It almost went wrong. Oh wait, and yesterday Mr Scribble said something in Egyptian and Dummie didn't understand it. It's going well but at the same time, not quite well enough."

Nick rubbed his chin. "Maybe it is all more complicated than I thought," he said. "Maybe I should show him what Egypt looks like today."

They went inside, Nick turned on the computer and showed Dummie what Egypt looked like now. Dummie had already seen it on the posters in the classroom, but Nick looked for some pictures of houses and markets. "If anyone asks, you should think of this," he said.

"Or don't say anything," Angus said. "That's the safest."

"I say just this," Dummie said.

"And about the language..." Nick continued to search. "Yes, here. The language Dummie spoke is probably just as much a relic as the hieroglyphics in the books. They speak modern Egyptian now. Hmm. Of course he doesn't understand that."

"So you shouldn't say anything about that either," Angus said. "Actually, just keep your mouth shut about everything. Understand, Dummie? Don't speak your own language. And don't say anything else about the pyramids being built."

"I get it," Dummie said. "I shut up."

"Alright," Nick said. He turned off the computer and stood up.

"And now about the hitting, Dad," Angus quickly added. "Dummie is much too hot-tempered."

Nick nodded and told Dummie he wasn't to hit anyone. "If anyone does anything you don't like, just keep your mouth shut. Walk the other way, then the bullying will stop."

But Dummie thought this was rubbish. "Do nothing doesn't ghelp," he said. "If she do bad, I ghit Annalisa."

"No. You can't," Nick said.

"Why not?" Dummie asked in surprise.

"Because you're not allowed to hit," Nick said.

"But she not allowed my can! Not allowed! If she do it, I ghit her ghead. Stupid child! Punish!" He got angrier the more he said. "I ghit her ghard. With stick! Lizzy too! I ghit everyone if need to. I am son of Akhnetut!"

"You used to be!" Nick said sternly. "Now you are here. Things are different here. You have to learn."

"I am son of Akhnetut!" Dummie shouted stubbornly. "I can ghit. And you must ghelp! Or I ghit you too!"

Nick looked at Dummie in amazement. Then he got up, picked up Dummie by his shoulders and shook him. "I am helping you! But there will be no hitting!" he said angrily. And when Dummie stared back just as angrily, he said, "If you hit anyone you won't be allowed to go to school. And now I'm going to fix that tyre." He got up and hurried out to the shed.

Angus took a deep breath. Had they fallen out? "Do you want to play chess?" he asked Dummie. And without waiting for a reply, he fetched the chessboard and set up all the pieces. When he'd finished, he looked Dummie in the face and then swiped all of the pieces from the board.

"You understand nothing," Dummie said crossly.

And neither do you, thought Angus.

When they arrived at school the next morning, Miss Frick was standing at the gate. When she spotted Angus and Dummie she rushed over to them. "I want to speak to you," she said sharply, her finger almost pointing through Dummie's flap. She grabbed him by the arm and dragged him inside.

Angus was shocked. Dummie had stayed angry the

entire evening and hadn't said a word, not even when Angus' father had sat down on his bed and gently told him that he did understand Dummie, but that he'd have to adapt to this day and age. Dummie had just rolled over and played with his scarab and Nick had left the room with a worried expression on his face.

Angus crept into the school and ran as quietly as he could to Miss Frick's office. He put his ear to the door.

"You must obey the rules," Miss Frick barked.

"I obey rules," came Dummie's voice.

"You are not to bully other children."

"I not bully," Dummie said.

"Yesterday you sprayed Annalisa with air freshener."

"She is wuss," Dummie said. He was angry, Angus could hear it.

"There will be no swearing here!" said Miss Frick. "I'm going to be keeping a beady eye on you. You are allowed here because I have permitted it, but if you upset other children, you will be out on your ear. Keep a low profile. Have you understood?"

"No," Dummie replied.

Angus gritted his teeth. Was the woman insane? She must realize that Dummie wouldn't understand all of that? And Dummie would have to just say "yes" to Miss Frick from now on. He'd drum that into him.

"Why did you have that air freshener with you, anyway?" Miss Frick snapped.

"Because I stink," Dummie snapped back.

Angus heard the sound of a zip opening.

"Give back! Is mine!" Dummie shouted.

"And now it's mine," Miss Frick said. "And what's

this? An empty lunchbox? An empty beaker?"

"Why have you got those?"

"I must from Nick," Dummie said. "All children ghave bag."

"Because all children eat!"

"I not!"

Angus felt suffocated. This conversation wasn't going well. Next Dummie would say he didn't eat because he didn't have a stomach. All of a sudden the bell went. Angus didn't hesitate and pushed open the door.

"And what are you doing here?" Miss Frick growled at him.

And what are you doing here?

"I've c-come to get Dummie. The l-lesson is about to start," Angus stuttered.

"Get out, the pair of you!" Miss Frick ordered. "And you..." she pointed a reprimanding finger at Dummie, "you have been warned!"

Dummie turned around and left the office without speaking. "That woman with ughly face is ughly wuss," he ranted in the hall. "She took my stink!" Miss Frick's sermon hadn't had any effect on him. He was just angry. And he certainly wasn't planning to keep a low profile. Firstly because he didn't understand what it meant and secondly because he didn't want to!

Luckily Annalisa and Lizzy were the class monitors that day and had to take the teachers their coffee and sweep the playground during the lunch break. That was one worry less, it didn't give them time to bully Dummie. Mr Scribble didn't mention Egypt at all and didn't say any Egyptian words. Dummie calmed down, did his best and played football during the break as happily as the day before. When the bell went, Angus sighed with relief. If he didn't count Miss Frick, the day had gone well.

Less than five minutes later, Angus realized he'd counted his blessings too soon. As he and Dummie walked over to the bikes, he saw that Dummie had a flat tyre again.

"Again broken flat," Dummie said.

"It's not possible," Angus said. "Those girls must have done it when they were sweeping the playground!" He was so indignant, he forgot that he wasn't supposed to make Dummie angry.

"Annalisa make my bike flat?" Dummie cried in a fit of rage. He strode over to Annalisa's light blue bike, picked up a sharp stone from the ground and before Angus could stop him, he'd sliced her front tyre down the middle.

"Stop!" Angus shouted, when Dummie made for her back wheel. He angrily dragged Dummie away and they ran across the playground with their bikes. Angus looked around. No one screaming at them, no sign of Annalisa. Whumpy dumpman. This whole school business with Dummie was coming badly unstuck!

When they arrived home, Nick behaved strangely. He didn't do anything when Angus told him that Dummie had shredded Annalisa's tyre. He didn't explode and he didn't begin to lecture them. He just shook his head, said that Dummie wasn't to do it again and repaired the tyre for a second time. After that, he took them to the petting zoo, without giving any explanation. Angus was much too old for it, but Dummie couldn't believe his eyes. All of the animals came and sniffed at Dummie curiously and he loved it. He lay down on his back and the rabbits jumped over him. Some goats nibbled at his bandages and even the chickens couldn't stay away from him.

They stayed for more than an hour. As they drove home, Dummie made animal noises in the car. "Aaa! Baaaa!" After that they took turns making animal noises and guessing which animal it was.

"Mooooo!"

"A cow."

"Quack quack!"

"Duck."

"Rraaargh!"

"Lion."

"And what's this?" Dummie asked as he shouted "blearrgghh!" at the top of his voice.

"A camel?" Nick guessed.

"Wrong! Angry mummy!" Dummie joked, roaring with laughter.

They had dinner, Nick turned on the television and the three of them watched a comedy. When it had finished, Nick took them to bed and read out a story for the first time in ages.

"I ghave song," Dummie said, when he'd finished. He softly began to sing an old Egyptian song. Angus listened to the cheerful melody and tried to copy it. The three of them continued to sing until they all knew the song off by heart. Dummie lay down in bed contentedly and got out his scarab. Nick stroked his head and gave Angus a kiss.

"Sleep tight," he said.

"Sleep tight," Angus and Dummie replied.

Dummie was asleep within five minutes. Angus wasn't. He got out of bed and went back downstairs.

Nick was in his red chair. "What's the matter?" he asked.

"What's the matter? Why weren't you cross with

Dummie?" Angus asked indignantly. "He sliced up her tyre and then we go off and have a nice time. That's not normal, is it? If I'd done something like that—"

"But you wouldn't do anything like that, because you've learned not to," Nick said. "Listen. We mustn't be angry with Dummie. We just have to teach him not to hit and not to break things, even if he thinks the other person deserves it. Even if he doesn't understand. But we also have to teach him that it's nice here. We showed him that today and I hope he understood."

Angus didn't understand. "But that tyre..." he said.

"The mayor will buy her a new one," Nick said drily. "Go back to bed. Everything will be alright."

Angus went back upstairs. If his father said so, it had to be true. But slicing a tyre wasn't good. You shouldn't take a kid to a petting zoo after that. It was insane.

As Angus and Dummie cycled onto the playground the next morning, a woman with pinned-up hair got out of a car. Angus knew who it was: it was Mrs Stickler, Annalisa's mother. This was because of the tyre! Mrs Stickler had seen them too. She gave Dummie a scornful look and went into the school.

Angus quickly locked his bike. "I want to know what she says. Come on," he said. He pulled Dummie inside and they headed for their classroom.

You could hear Mrs Sticklers" voice from the corridor. She had a high-pitched voice which could sound very posh, but right now she was snarling.

"The whole tyre sliced through!" Mrs Stickler snarled.

"That is annoying, indeed," Mr Scribble said.

"Annoying? It's mindless vandalism! This is what happens when you allow foreigners into the school!"

"Do you mean Dummie?" Mr Scribble asked in a suspiciously calm voice.

"Is that what that Egyptian boy is called? I meant him, yes."

"And why do you think it was him?"

"Who else would it be? Someone from our own village? Don't make me laugh."

Mr Scribble carried on calmly and Angus was pretty impressed by this. "Perhaps your daughter ran over a piece of glass. Had you thought of that?"

"No! Of course not! My daughter never runs over glass!"

"Really? Well, I do sometimes," Mr Scribble countered.

"What do I care? You should be more careful. Annalisa's tyre was deliberately vandalized and I want you to find out who did it."

"Mrs Stickler, I think a piece of glass did it. There is no proof that it was anything else, so I'm going to leave it at that," Mr Scribble said. "If you'll excuse me, I need to begin your daughter's lesson and I think that's more important than arresting a piece of glass." He must have looked at the clock, because at that exact moment the bell went. They heard chairs being pushed back and Angus and Dummie shot back out of the school. Out of the corner of his eye, Angus saw Mrs Stickler stamping across the playground. Mr Scribble had made her furious. That served her right, Angus thought. At least the teacher was on their side.

The rest of the morning passed without incident because Mr Scribble kept a sharp eye on Annalisa. When she went to the bathroom, he followed her into the corridor as though he had to fetch something. But Angus thought he was just checking that she really did need to pee.

Dummie sat there scribbling away and doing his sums. He had paid attention the entire week and was already on his second maths book. At the end of the morning Angus let out another sigh of relief.

At lunchtime, Mr Scribble came and sat with Angus and Dummie in the assembly hall. Angus thought it was his way of keeping Annalisa away from Dummie, but after they'd eaten he asked them to stay back. He waited until all the other children had left and then said, "Annalisa's mother was here. She mentioned a flat tyre."

"I ghave done it," Dummie said at once. "She made my tyre flat. Two times. I cannot ghit from Nick. But I am angry."

Mr Scribble nodded. "I thought so," he said. "But you're not allowed to do things like that."

"She not too," Dummie said.

"Yes, you're right." Mr Scribble leaned back. He wanted to say something but didn't seem to know how to. "Listen," he began. "Most people mean well. But some people only think of themselves. They don't like other people. And particularly not if they, erm... are different, like you. You have to try to ignore it. And don't let it upset you. Do you understand?"

"But they do it," Dummie said.

"Because they are stupid," Mr Scribble said. "But you're not stupid, are you?"

"No. I am ghood," Dummie said.

"Exactly," Mr Scribble said. "And that's why you are going to manage it. And I am going to help you. And now go out and kick a ball around, both of you."

He followed them outside and sat down on a bench at the side of the playground. Annalisa and Lizzy were at the climbing frame and looked in their direction. They knew why Mr Scribble was sitting there. Their faces got even nastier than they usually were, but they couldn't do anything about Mr Scribble.

Angus and Dummie played football and soon it was one o'clock. Just one more afternoon and it'd be the weekend, Angus thought.

And then, on that Friday afternoon, Dummie did something stupid. Something very stupid. He took out his scarab.

It happened before Angus had realized. Mr Scribble had hung up a poster of the sacred animals in ancient Egypt and the class had to learn them off by heart. They'd already gone through this twice, but Mr Scribble wanted to make sure that his class won the schools' competition and so he kept on repeating everything all the time. He pointed at the pictures with a stick and the class chanted the answers.

"Cat. Snake. Apis bull. Falcon."

Mr Scribble pointed his stick at the beetle. "And this is a...?"

"Scarab," the class answered in chorus.

At once Dummie reached his hand inside his bandages and pulled out his scarab. "I ghave too," he said.

Angus almost fell off his chair. Mr Scribble stared at the golden object. Everyone stared at the golden object.

"Wow," Ebbi muttered.

"This is real scarab," Dummie said proudly. "From my country."

"Well, that's quite impressive," Mr Scribble said finally. "Could I take a closer look at it?"

"No," Dummie said and put his scarab away again under his bandages.

Angus looked around. The entire class was staring at Dummie's chain. Angus was terrified someone would ask about it. How Dummie got it, for example. And that Dummie would say it had be given to him before he died. But no one said a thing and Mr Scribble just carried on with his poster.

Angus had to go to the bathroom in the break and Dummie went outside into the playground with the others. Angus had finished and was about to open the door when he heard whispering on the other side.

"See, he is bad," came the sound of Annalisa's voice. "He must have stolen it. A boy like that isn't rich. My mother was right. That stink-bag shouldn't be allowed in our school."

"Mr Scribble thinks he should," Lizzy said hesitantly.

"Mr Scribble's got it in for us. All he thinks about is that stupid competition," Annalisa said. "And the rest just feel sorry for him because of his burns. Pfff. As though that makes someone honest. We'll have to get rid of him on our own, before he robs us too."

Angus exploded. He threw open the toilet door and looked at them as though he wanted to feed them to the crocodiles.

"I heard all of that," he raged.

"Congratulations then," Annalisa chuntered. "You can go and warn that dumbo stink-bag."

Angus stormed outside, even angrier. To make matters worse, the class was standing in a circle around Dummie at the climbing frame. Dummie had pulled out his scarab for the second time and was letting them all touch it. Whumpy dumpman! Had Dummie gone mad? Angus pushed his way angrily into the circle. Dummie was strutting like a peacock and the children were all saying that the scarab was the prettiest thing they'd ever seen. Finally Dummie put the scarab back under his bandages and they played soccer.

When they went back inside, the lesson started at once. It was a drawing lesson and the class all found Dummie even more wonderful because he could draw better than all of the others put together. "You're as good as Rembrandt!" Ebbi cried out in admiration.

It seemed like an eternity before it turned three o'clock and the class emptied. "Bye Dummie! Have a good weekend!" some children called out. Dummie waved cheerfully and got onto his bike, which didn't have a flat tyre today. Finally Angus was alone with Dummie. "How could you do that?" he shouted. "How could you be stupid enough to let them see your scarab?"

"Everyone has chain. Me too. Not bad."

"It is bad!"

"Why?"

"Because— because—" Well, why exactly? Why was he so angry about it? Because of what Annalisa had said? Or because he was afraid Dummie would stand out even more with the scarab?

Dummie looked away. Angus could see his eyes glowing through the flap. "Who's Rembrandt?" he asked.

"Who cares. A painter," Angus snapped.

"Like Nick?"

"No. Better," Angus said.

"So I am better than Nick," Dummie said proudly.

"No. Shut up!"

"He showed them his scarab," Angus told his father. "And now Annalisa thinks he's a thief."

To his astonishment his father didn't seem bothered by this. "They'd have seen it sooner or later anyway," Nick said. "The fewer secrets, the better."

"Dummie is still one big secret, you know," Angus said huffily.

"Yes. But the scarab isn't now, and that makes it easier. How did it go apart from that?"

"Mrs Stickler came to school to complain about that tyre. Mr Scribble sent her away again, but gave us a warning later. He said that not everyone's nice. If Mr Scribble knew too, that Dummie's a mummy, he could help us. I think we could tell him." He'd only just come up with the idea. If there was anyone they could trust, it was Mr Scribble. "Then he won't ask the wrong questions anymore. Isn't that a good idea, Dad?"

Nick thought about it. "I don't think so," he said. "Let's enjoy the weekend first. A good weekend always makes Monday look better."

Angus rolled his eyes. These days he didn't seem to agree with his father as much as he used to. Though he might be right about enjoying the weekend. Two days without Annalisa, Lizzy and Miss Frick and no posters about Egypt.

So they enjoyed the weekend.

First they went kite-flying. Nick had bought a kite and showed Dummie how it worked. There was a strong wind and the kite swooped down at top speed and turned and sometimes just missed the ground. Dummie loved it, until he steered the kite into a tree and it got stuck right at the top. Of course Dummie clambered up after it, but when he was halfway, the kite suddenly shot back into the air and disappeared. Angus was rather relieved, because if Dummie had fallen out of such a tall tree, his head really might have come off.

In the evening, Dummie wanted to watch the same film as the day before, so they went to bed late.

Nick had thought of fun activities for the rest of the weekend too. Now that Dummie no longer had to hide, he could just come with them in the car. Angus and his father never went anywhere, but Nick wanted to teach Dummie all about the Netherlands, so on Saturday they drove to the beach. They built a sandcastle and lying on a beach towel, they taught Dummie words like windbreak and parasol and waves. Angus went swimming, but Dummie didn't want to come. And when they had ice-creams, Dummie had nothing. But next they went trampolining and Dummie was unstoppable. He bounced up and down until a whole group of people had surrounded the trampoline. The people watched the bandaged boy open-mouthed and whispered, "oh, how awful," and "amazing he can do that," and that kind of thing. Nick mentioned to a few people that Dummie had bad burns, but that they didn't hurt anymore and then they all thought Dummie amazing. They clapped until their hands turned red and Dummie was allowed three goes for free, because all of the children on the beach suddenly wanted to jump with him.

On Sunday they went to the woods. They didn't meet anyone there. And that was good, because Dummie climbed up all the trees and broke his neck at least three times without showing any pain. No one would have believed that.

On Sunday evening all three of them were tired.

Angus felt a bit happier, he was almost looking forward to going back to school. He saw his father smile. He had been right. After an enjoyable weekend, Monday did look better, like he'd said. Even on Sunday evening!

On Monday morning, Angus discovered that Dummie really was allergic to water.

They went to school early and were the first to turn up on the playground. Angus saw it straight away. *DUMMIE IS A THIEF!* Written in chalk in the middle of the playground. Annalisa, Angus thought. The scarab.

Dummie looked at it and balled his hands into fists. Then he went into the school, got the chalk from the classroom and knelt down. He began to draw with large strokes. While he was busy, more and more children arrived. "What's he doing? What's he doing?"

they cried. A circle formed around him and they were all pushing and shoving to get a better look.

Finally Dummie got up and all the children could see what he had done. He'd turned the letters of his name into a big ball of curls and underneath he'd drawn a face. Everyone could see at once who it was: Annalisa. He'd written her name and now it said *ANNALISA IS A THIEF!*

Satisfied with his work, he dusted off his hands and returned the chalk. Angus quickly told the others that at first it had said *DUMMIE IS A THIEF!* They all began to whisper and a few children clapped. "Serves her right," someone said. But Angus was thinking, oh no, here we go again. And the week hadn't even begun yet.

It wasn't long before Miss Frick stormed over with a bucket of water and a broom. She put her hands in her sides and looked at the drawing.

"Who did this?" she snarled.

"I ghave done it," Dummie said, right behind her. "First it say: *DUMMIE IS A THIEF!* I am not thief!"

Miss Frick thrust the broom into Dummie's hands and said, "Get cleaning! I won't allow this to stay here! Annalisa is not a thief!"

"I too not!" Dummie said.

"But Annalisa is the mayor's daughter!"

Dummie looked at her angrily and said, "So what! I am son of phar—"

Angus began to scream. He didn't know what else to do. Everyone looked at him in shock. "A wasp!" he screamed. "A wasp in my mouth!"

Dummie was just as shocked. He turned around

and then it happened. He kicked the bucket over and water streamed over his foot. Dummie froze, looked down and began to shriek. "No! No!" he screamed. He lifted up his wet foot and hopped away from the water. "No! Ghelp! No!"

"What's the matter?" Angus cried in concern.

"My foot not. Water not!"

Angus' mind raced. Was Dummie allergic to water? Did it hurt him? That's why he didn't want to be washed and didn't want to go swimming! "It's because of his wounds!" he cried out. "Who's going to help with the cleaning?" And he grabbed the brush and began to scrub as hard as he could. Ebbi joined in and Dummie stood watching them on one leg, jabbering away. To make matters worse, Annalisa and Lizzy turned up. They gave Dummie a curious look, but he just kept on hopping and crying out that his foot couldn't go in the water. Angus could hear them all thinking that Dummie was scared of water!

When the playground was clean again, they went inside. Dummie hopped along after them and sank groaning into his chair. Mr Scribble bent down over him in concern, but Dummie said, "Don't touch. Don't do it. Foot must dry."

So Mr Scribble left him alone and started the lesson.

Dummie didn't get up from his chair for the rest of the day. Only at lunchtime did he hop to the assembly hall to pretend to eat. But he didn't play football and he didn't speak. Annalisa and Lizzy kept on staring at him. Angus could hear Annalisa's voice in his head. We'll just have to get rid of him on our own, she'd said.

And now she knew that Dummie hated water. Nick's enjoyable weekend seemed like years ago.

Luckily Dummie's foot improved somewhat during the afternoon and at three o'clock he was able to stand on it again.

"Does water hurt?" Angus asked, as they cautiously cycled home.

"Not hurt but bad," Dummie said. "Water go through bandage. Leg goes away through bandage."

"Your leg goes away? What do you mean, away? How do you know that?"

"I ghave seen it," Dummie said. "In mummy of cat. Nile was angry and sent much water. Also to cave with cat mummy. Cat mummy wet. Then cat went away. Only bandage left, all brown. Cat gone. Can't get wet."

Angus' mind raced. Had there been a great flood in the past during which Dummie had seen a cat mummy that had dissolved? And could that happen to Dummie too? Was Dummie a kind of gigantic sugar lump? Well that was just brilliant! They cycled along a canal every day. They were risking his life! And there was a river close to their house! All of a sudden Angus could see water everywhere. Whumpy dumpman! Their whole country was covered in water!

At home, Angus immediately explained what had happened, and Nick was keen to check under the bandages. He knelt down, peeled the bandage from Dummie's foot and pulled a face as he looked at the bones and bits of loose skin. Dummie's foot wasn't completely dry yet and he stank.

"I think he's still whole," Nick muttered. "We'll

let him dry and I think it'll be fine after that." He rested Dummie's foot up on a chair and turned on the television.

The foot was dry before dinner and they wrapped it up carefully again. "Walk around a bit," Nick said. Dummie did a turn of the living room. "Can you jump?" Dummie climbed onto the table and jumped onto Nick's neck. "Ghop, ghop," he cried.

"Ouch! I'm not a camel!" Nick said angrily.

Angus could laugh again. Well. Everything kept going wrong, but it kept turning out alright in the end too.

From that day onwards, Angus kept an eye out for water. It became a habit. He was always looking around for water, anywhere Dummie might dissolve. He also kept an eye out for buckets, beakers, containers of water. He was sure that Annalisa and Lizzy would use their new weapon.

When they went back inside after the break, he spotted a plastic bag hanging on the peg underneath Annalisa's coat. He shoved Dummie into the classroom and hurried back to it. There were two big water pistols in the bag. Annalisa and Lizzy had brought water pistols to school! Well, now they'd lost them, what a shame. Angus grabbed the bag, looked around and to his horror, saw Miss Frick coming towards him. He quickly hid the bag behind his back but she had already seen it. "What's in the bag?" she asked sharply.

"Erm... water pistols. They're Annalisa and Lizzy's," Angus replied, blushing.

She came down on him like a tonne of bricks. He shouldn't take other children's things, he was becoming almost as much as a thief as his burned Egyptian friend.

Angus felt something snap. "Annalisa and Lizzy want to squirt Dummie with water because he hates it. It's horrible and mean! They are horrible and mean!"

Miss Frick raised her nose in the air and instantly looked like a pig. "Shut your cheeky, little mouth!" she snarled. "It's warm and they aren't the only children who want to bring water pistols for lunchtime. There's nothing mean about it!"

"I told you, they want to squirt Dummie! You have to confiscate the pistols. You have to punish them!" Angus screamed.

"I don't have to do anything," she snorted. "You have to do something. Stop screaming! And stay away from other people's things! Put it back! Now!"

The door of Angus' classroom opened and Mr Scribble poked his head around the corner. "What's going on?" he asked.

"I caught the Egyptian's little friend. He was about to steal something. I want you to keep a better eye on those two. There's no place for thieves in this school. Inside with you, hurry!"

Angus hung the bag back up, went into the classroom, on the verge of exploding.

Mr Scribble began the lesson. He looked at Angus'

furious face from time to time and winked at him twice. When the bell went for the break, he kept him back.

"What was that all about?" he asked in concern.

Angus looked at Dummie who was already on his way out. He quickly told him about the water pistols and that Miss Frick had called him a thief. "I'm not a thief," he said angrily. "I have to go outside now. I have to look out for Annalisa. She wants to squirt Dummie. I'm off."

Mr Scribble nodded and let him go.

Angus kept Annalisa and Lizzy in his sights for the rest of the day. He didn't play football in the break but just hung around them. It made them as unhappy as it made him, but at least it worked.

At last it was three o'clock. Angus waited until Annalisa and Lizzy had left the playground before getting onto his bike. He was just feeling relieved when it all went wrong.

They were leaving the

playground when all of a sudden, Dummie shouted out, "No!"

Angus looked at him in shock. There was a wet patch in the middle of Dummie's face.

SPLAT! A water balloon bounced off Dummie's head and there was a second wet patch. And another one. And another one.

"No! No!" Dummie cried in panic. He got off his bike, ducked down and held his hands in front of his face.

Angus turned around furiously. Annalisa and Lizzy were standing behind a tree, throwing water balloons at Dummie. Angus didn't hesitate for a second, he rushed over to them and grabbed the bag of balloons. "Don't be so mean! You're hurting him!" he screamed.

Annalisa and Lizzy ran off laughing. "It's only water!" Annalisa called back. Angus balled his fists, ran back to Dummie and looked at his head. There were four brown patches on the bandage, two on his forehead and two on his cheek. "Does it hurt?" he asked.

"No! But my ghead! Must not get wet!"

Angus was overcome with white hot rage. And his father would be too.

Once Angus had told him the whole story, Nick began to pace around the room with heavy footsteps. "Will the bullying never stop?" he cried angrily.

"Are we still supposed to just ignore it?" Angus asked, bad-temperedly.

"Yes. No. I'm calling her mother." Nick picked up the phone and the phone book. A few seconds later he had Mrs Stickler on the line. He tried to stay calm, but in less than a minute he was shouting. "What? How dare you? Only water? You have no idea what you're talking about. Oh, go fly a kite!" He hung up and turned around, still furious.

"What did she say?" Angus asked.

"That it was only a practical joke. And that anyone who can't cope with water doesn't belong here!" Nick raged. "Has that woman gone stark raving mad? I'd like to give her a big smack! I'd like to beat her from top to—" He shut his mouth again and looked at Angus in shock.

Angus was shocked too. He'd never seen his father get this angry.

"No, I won't do that," Nick added quickly. His shoulders slumped and he sat down. "Do you know how hard I'm trying?" he said, suddenly tired. "We're all doing our best and a couple of idiots are ruining it all. And for what?"

Angus didn't know either. "Mr Scribble said that some people don't like people who are different," he said.

"Oh, whatever!" Nick sighed. "We'll just keep going," he said then. "We'll be even more careful. It can't go on forever. They'll get tired of it."

"When will they?" Angus asked.

"When I ghit them," Dummie said. He hadn't said anything up to this point. He had only listened. "I am fed up. I am going to ghit. They are enemy."

"Yes, and then we'll play football with their heads, I bet," Nick said. He was only joking but Dummie nodded. He was deadly serious.

"Good. First I cut off her big ghair," he said. The three of them had to laugh at that.

"Let's play a game," Nick said finally.

They played Monopoly, ate potatoes with broccoli and went to bed on time, without discussing it again.

That night, Angus had a horrible nightmare. He was cycling down the road with Dummie. Suddenly a large fire engine came towards them. It screeched to a halt in front of them. Annalisa and Lizzy jumped off wearing helmets and red suits. They unrolled a fire hose and pointed it at Dummie. Shrieking with pleasure, they turned it on. They didn't stop until Dummie had completely dissolved and there was only a pile of bandages and a large brown puddle left. Angus woke up sweating and didn't dare go back to sleep.

On Thursday it happened.

Mr Scribble had told the children on Wednesday that no one was allowed to bring water pistols to school because they only caused arguments. He must have spoken to Annalisa and Lizzy too, because they sat there looking cross and kept their heads down all day.

But on Thursday everything went wrong. On Thursday, Dummie got so angry he did the most stupid thing he could have done. Angus understood why, those girls had driven him to distraction. But still, Dummie shouldn't have done it.

It happened at the end of the morning.

The children were tidying away their maths books when Annalisa's pencil case fell on the floor. She said, "oops," sunk down in her chair and began to crawl around on the floor, picking up the pencils that had escaped. A couple had rolled towards Dummie's table so she was fumbling around near him too. Angus pretended not to see her and was mainly checking that Dummie didn't give her a good kick. It wasn't until afterwards that he realised this was when she must have done it.

When the bell went, Annalisa stood up, got a water pistol out of her bag, pointed it at Dummie and said provocatively, "See this?" Dummie saw the gun, jumped up and then smacked down onto the floor. He grabbed at his leg with a cry. Angus choked. Annalisa had tied a bit of Dummie's bandage to the chair leg. A large piece of white bandage had rolled from his leg and Dummie own, brown bandages could be seen underneath. But that wasn't the worst. The worst thing was that Dummie's old bandage had been pulled up and a bit of Dummie's leg was showing. Someone began to scream. Angus looked around and saw that the whole class was staring at Dummie's leg. Quick as a flash, he threw himself to the ground and bound the leg up again. But everybody had seen it! Everybody had seen Dummie's leg!

Dummie exploded. He jumped to his feet, tore over to Annalisa and pulled her head back by her hair. And then he did the worst thing he could do. While Annalisa was screaming like she was being murdered, Dummie held his face close to hers and lifted up his flap. "sɪRꜱAR!" he hissed.

Annalisa turned pale. Now she began to scream so loudly that it was a wonder the windows didn't break. "Waaaah! A monster!" she screamed.

Angus quickly pulled Dummie away, but it was already too late. Annalisa had seen his face. Angus looked around anxiously. No one else had seen it, otherwise they would have all screamed, at least the girls would have. But that stupid, mean Annalisa had seen that Dummie was a mummy. Their secret was out. Now everything would come out.

All of a sudden, Mr Scribble's hand appeared. He pulled Dummie away from Annalisa and began to thunder. "Have you gone completely mad?" he shouted at Annalisa.

Annalisa sobbed. "He's a monster! There's a monster in our class! I'm going to faint!"

She didn't faint, because when you faint you stop talking. In any case, Mr Scribble didn't feel sorry for her in the slightest. He was furious. His eyes were ablaze, he raised his hand and it looked for a moment as though he might hit her.

"Stand in the corner! Lines!" he fumed. "How dare you call Dummie that? Burns like that are terrible!"

"But he really is a monster!"

"Shut up!" Mr Scribble roared.

Annalisa shut up. She sat down at the table in the corner of the classroom, wrote her lines and didn't say anything else.

At lunchtime she went home and didn't come back.

Angus was a mess. Not because of Dummie's leg. Everyone who'd seen it was whispering about the horrible scars left from the fire. No one was talking about dried-up mummy flesh, Angus would have heard it. But Annalisa had seen Dummie's face.

Without a nose and with those big, golden eyes. She had called him a monster, because he looked like a monster. And she had seen it!

"Why did you do that?" Angus cried out as soon as they were outside in the break. "She's seen you. She knows now! You idiot! Now they'll come and take you away!"

"So you want I like it?" Dummie snorted back at him, just as angry.

"No. But that was... that was just stupid! You'll be sent away from school!"

"No. I did not ghit," Dummie said stubbornly.

No. This was ten times worse! Angus looked at him, speechless. What was he supposed to say? That it had all been for nothing? Dummie had brains, didn't he? How could he have been so stupid?!

That afternoon, after school, Mrs Stickler was waiting in the playground.

"I want to hear what she says. I have to know," Angus said to Dummie. So they hid in the toilets until everyone had left and then peered through a chink in the door until Mrs Stickler stormed past. She hurried towards their classroom and went in. Angus and Dummie hurried after her to listen at the door.

"This is the second time this week I've had to come to the school!" Mrs Stickler said in her shrill voice. "All because of that boy! I demand he will be punished!

He won't stop. First he wrote on the playground that Annalisa was a thief, and now he has pulled her hair. He deliberately showed her his burn wounds. He scared the death out of her. That boy is just bad inside!"

Dummie balled his fists. But Angus couldn't believe his ears. She'd said 'burn wounds'. Annalisa had told her mother she'd seen his burn wounds. Not a mummy. He began to feel more hopeful.

Mr Scribble's voice sounded less friendly than the previous time. "Your daughter tied his bandages to a table, making Dummie fall over," he said in a stern voice.

"That was a joke," Mrs Stickler snarled.

"It was a joke that backfired, no one thought it was funny."

"Children pull those kinds of pranks," Mrs Stickler said. "It doesn't mean—"

"It's not the right kind of humour," Mr Scribble interrupted her.

Mrs Stickler's voice got even nastier than it already was. "Just you listen to me, Mr Scribble. I insist that you guarantee my daughter's safety at school. No one pulls my daughter's hair. And certainly not some kind of—"

"Yes?" Mr Scribble asked, much too friendlily. He was about to explode, Angus was sure.

"... dirty, stinking foreigner!" Mrs Stickler said. "And if you ask me, he's a thief too. How did that boy afford a gold necklace? That kind of boy doesn't belong at our school!"

Now Angus was balling his fists too. Who did that

horrid person think she was? He almost felt sorry for Annalisa. How could you be nice with a mother like that?

For a while there was silence. Then Mr Scribble said something very slowly and very clearly. "My dear Mrs Stickler. I believe you have made yourself clear. Dummie is in my class and he is not better nor worse than your daughter. Annalisa bullied Dummie and Dummie fought back. Now they are even. I will talk to them both and then we're done with this business. Goodbye."

There was another silence. Maybe Mrs Stickler had had a fainting fit, Angus thought. But she hadn't because he suddenly heard screaming. "I won't leave it at this! I'm going to see Miss Frick!"

Angus turned around and quickly pulled Dummie with him into the toilets. Three seconds later, Mrs Stickler stomped past.

Angus and Dummie went home and Angus told his father everything. Nick grew pale, but when Angus told him that they all still thought that Dummie had burns wounds, even Annalisa who had seen his face (or what was left of it), he let out a sigh of relief. "Whumpy dumpman, you really are making a mess of things," he said to Dummie. He began to explain yet again why Dummie couldn't let them see him. "It will all go wrong. You won't be able to stay with us. And you won't ever go to school again either."

"I know," Dummie said crossly after each sentence.

"Why do you do it then?" Nick asked.

"Because I angry!" Dummie said. "When I angry I do that."

There was no arguing with him. And to be honest, Angus understood Dummie. Dummie just had a much worse temper than he did.

Nick paced up and down a bit. Angus saw him thinking. They'd made it through another day, but this time only just. He stood in front of Dummie and gripped his shoulders. "Dummie," he began insistently, "this really is your final warning. If you lose your temper again, I'll take you out of school. I will do it, because I have to. There isn't any other way, do you hear? I really mean it."

Dummie got up without saying anything else and went upstairs.

The next morning, Miss Frick was waiting for Dummie in the playground for the second time. This time she didn't take him to her office but began to rant at him in the middle of the playground. Perhaps she wanted everyone to hear what she was saying. And it was quite something.

Dummie was a show-off with his golden pendant, she said. He scared the children to death. Tyres had been deliberately punctured and he had insulted children by writing on the playground that they were thieves. Since he'd arrived, the peace had been disturbed at the school.

Then she bent down to him and snarled, "I'm giving you one last chance and get this into your scorched ears. If you bother anyone again, we're done with you.

All of the other children have been here longer than you. Whether they're nice to you or not, you have to be the one to fit in. You will show respect and you will behave yourself. Otherwise it's finished."

She had said what she wanted to say, she stood up straight and looked around almost triumphantly.

Ebbi raised his hand. "May I say something?" he asked.

Miss Frick gave him an irritated look. "What is it?"

"Annalisa and Lizzy have been bullying Dummie ever since he first got here," Ebbi said. "Of course Dummie gets cross. And the whole class does too. We're not allowed to bully people, are we? We have to help him!" He adopted an innocent expression to top it all off.

Miss Frick opened and closed her mouth. Angus bit his lip. Ebbi had been brilliant. How was she going to reply to that? She could hardly say that bullying was good.

"There will be no bullying here," she said at last. "Not by anyone." Then she walked off.

That Friday nobody bothered Dummie. They made it to the weekend without anything else happening.

The scarab of Makatagara

After the weekend, something terrible happened.

Monday began like a normal school day. It was warm and Mr Scribble to decided to have the gym lesson outside. All the children could practise a trick on the climbing frame and then show it to the others.

Dummie ran along the top bar without holding on, hung upside down from it and then swung backwards and forwards until he'd done a full turn.

Because it was too hot to play football, they played hide and seek in the break. All of the children joined in and Dummie hid so well that no one could find him. He even climbed into the large rubbish bin in the playground and gave Ebbi such a fright that he remained paler than a cauliflower for five whole minutes.

At lunchtime they played it again. Now Dummie wanted to be the seeker and he found everyone easily by climbing up onto the roof, which allowed him to see where they all were.

To Angus' surprise, Annalisa and Lizzy spent the day acting as though Dummie didn't exist. Maybe the bullying was over at last, he thought to himself in relief.

After school, Dummie and Angus cycled home in good spirits. Angus made a drink in the kitchen and Dummie turned on the TV.

All of a sudden, Angus heard a scream. He ran into the sitting room, terrified.

Dummie was standing next to the sofa, feeling all over his bandages. "Scarab!" he cried. "My scarab is gone!"

"What?"

"I lost scarab. No! Not possible! Scarab is gone!"

Angus looked under Dummie's bandages on his back and then all over his body. He didn't find anything. "When did you last see it?" he asked in concern.

"I don't know. Ghere. At school. Always," Dummie jabbered.

"Did you take it off?"

"No!"

"Did you show it to anyone again?"

"No! Ghe is gone! Not possible! Not possible!"

As Dummie began to wail louder and louder, Angus

ran into the shed to fetch his father.

"It might be somewhere in the house. We played hide and seek yesterday," Nick said. So the three of them searched the entire house. When they still hadn't found the scarab they cycled to school and searched the grass, the pavement, the bushes, everywhere on the way.

They didn't find a thing.

Nick called the police station and asked if anyone had handed in any gold jewellery. "Round, yes. Quite big. A golden beetle, on an iron chain." Nick hung up and shook his head. "Nothing," he said.

"Then it must be at school, we played hide and seek there," Angus said. So they went back to the school. It was almost five o'clock and the school was already closed. They searched all over the playground: under the climbing frame, in the bushes and Dummie climbed up onto the roof again because he'd been there as well. They even turned the bin inside out, but they didn't find anything.

At home, they began a new search. Now they turned the whole house upside down, they looked under pans, flower pots and vases, moved everything from its place and even looked inside the freezer. Nick emptied the vacuum cleaner bag and peered into the oven. They went through everything in the attic and found lots of things they'd forgotten they had. A bag containing a tent, an old chain, a ring that Nick had lost. Nick must have hit his head ten times, and shouted out "Whumpy dumpman" just as often and the attic got completely tidied up, but the golden scarab was still missing.

Defeated, they went to sit in the bedroom. Dummie was inconsolable. He just kept on crying without any tears coming out. It made Angus feel terrible. The scarab was the only thing Dummie had left from his mother and father. And now he'd lost it...

"Shall we buy a new chain for you?" Nick asked, after a while.

"No," Dummie said despondently. "I need my scarab. Scarab of Mukatagara!" He stopped crying and sat silently staring ahead. He looked so sad that Angus almost started crying too. But he didn't know what to do. And his father didn't either. So they didn't do anything. Nick went off to cook potatoes and broccoli, they ate and then turned on the television. Dummie didn't even look at the screen. And after half an hour of not watching he went to bed on his own.

"Shouldn't we do something?" Angus asked in a worried voice.

"It'll pass," Nick said. "He's lost something very important to him. That's terrible, but it will pass. It takes time. After a while he'll start to think about it less, and then he'll get used to it."

"How long does that take?" Angus asked.

"The longer you have had something, the longer it takes," his father replied.

Well, that was brilliant. Dummie had had the scarab for more than four thousand years!

Angus went upstairs and found Dummie in bed with the covers over his head. Angus sat down next to him and rubbed the covers at the place Dummie's shoulders should be. "Hey, Dummie," he said.

Dummie didn't respond so Angus got into bed too. Nick came up and did exactly the same as Angus. After that he scratched his chin indecisively, said goodnight and went back down again.

Angus looked over and felt guilty. He knew that Dummie was a daredevil. He should have looked after him better. And the scarab. Or had the chain simply snapped? All of a sudden something flashed through his mind. Maybe Dummie hadn't lost the scarab. Maybe it had been stolen! It was big and made of gold and worth lots of money. Everyone at school knew about the scarab because Dummie had showed them himself. Annalisa! If it was stolen, Annalisa was the number one suspect. She hated Dummie and wanted to bully him until he left. But bullying wasn't theft. And she was the mayor's daughter. The mayor's daughter wouldn't steal, would she? You couldn't really steal it either. A thief would have to get it out from under the bandages first and then pull it over Dummie's head. Dummie would have definitely noticed. So the scarab can't have been stolen. Or could it?

Blasting cackdingle!

The next morning Dummie didn't feel well.
"I don't go downstairs. I don't feel good," he said.
Angus studied him. Dummie looked just as brown as usual, but his golden eyes were dull.

"Didn't you sleep well?" Angus asked.

"No. Because of scarab," Dummie said. "I stay ghome."

Angus brushed his teeth and went downstairs. "Dummie doesn't want to go to school. He's not feeling well," he told his father.

"I understand. He can stay home today," Nick said. "You can go on your own."

So Angus cycled to school on his own. He locked his bike and looked around. Someone might be acting suspiciously. But everyone asked where Dummie was with concern and when Angus said that Dummie was ill, they all felt sorry for him. "I feel sorry for us too," said Ebbi, "Dummie's so much fun." Everybody agreed and they all seemed so genuine that no one was suspicious. Only Annalisa smiled when she heard that Dummie was ill, and her eyes said, "serves him right". But was that suspicious? It would have been more suspicious if she'd said she hoped he got better soon.

Angus went into the school and told Mr Scribble that Dummie was ill. Mr Scribble didn't find it strange, a flu bug was going around, he said, and three other children in the class were ill.

He started the lesson and the day crept onwards. Angus didn't say anything about the scarab and kept his eyes peeled, but nothing noticeable happened. During the breaks he searched for the scarab inside the school building, he even looked in the toilets, where Dummie never needed to go. But he didn't find it.

When school was out, Angus raced home. Maybe Dummie would have cheered up. He might be sitting in the shed with his father, drawing, like when he first arrived. Or he might be secretly wrecking the vacuum cleaner, also fine. But Angus found Dummie lying on his bed.

"How are you?" he asked, concerned.

"I don't feel good. I miss scarab," Dummie said. His eyes were still dull and he was just lying there.

"Come on, let's play chess," Angus suggested. Playing chess with Dummie wasn't much fun anymore, not since he'd understood how to play it. Now he always won. But not today. Dummie played appallingly and within five minutes, Angus had beaten him.

"Check mate," Angus said.

"OK. You ghave won," Dummie said before lying back down on his bed.

Angus went and sat next to him. Dummie was lying there like a ragdoll.

"What's the matter exactly?" Angus asked.

"I miss scarab," Dummie whispered. Then he did something he'd never done in the house before. He closed his flap. Angus was worried. Was Dummie mad at him? Did he think that he should have taken better care of the scarab? Was he blaming him? "Hey, Dummie. I'll find it for you. Honestly," he said. Dummie didn't respond. Blasting cackdingle. Feeling totally confused, Angus went back downstairs.

Nick was painting in the shed. He seemed confused too because the mess he was making wasn't anything he could ever sell.

"Hey, Angus, is it that late already?" he said, taken

aback. "How was school?"

"Dummie really doesn't feel well," Angus said. "And he seems angry. He put his flap down."

Nick dried his brushes absent-mindedly. "I know," he said. "He just keeps going on about the scarab."

Then Angus had a very worrying idea. It was as though someone was choking him, he felt so suffocated. Dummie's words shot through his head like a lightning strike. "I can't without scarab. Without scarab I am dead."

"Dad, could... could... could it have to do with the scarab? That he gets ill without it?" he asked.

Nick looked him in the eye. Angus hoped that he'd say it was nonsense and that everyone got sick from time to time, even someone who was already dead. But his father said, "I've thought about that too, son. All day in fact." That made Angus even more worried.

They went into the house and Angus couldn't think of anything to do apart from sitting in his room with a book. But he didn't read a word, just stared at the bump under Dummie's bedclothes. Dummie hadn't used the toilet freshener today, he stank of rotten eggs and dead mice.

Angus and Nick ate in silence and Dummie wanted to go back upstairs right away. He was ill, he said, and he felt cold. Angus laid his hand on Dummie's head and he did feel cold. Angus shivered. "Are you sure he can't have flu, Dad? It's going around," said Angus. "Then it will clear up on its own, won't it? We'll just wait for that, won't we, Dad?"

His father nodded and said, "We'll just wait for

that, son." But Angus could see from his face that he
didn't believe it. His throat tightened again. What if it
wasn't the flu? What if Dummie got more ill? What if
he really couldn't do without his scarab? No! He didn't
want to think about it!

When Angus went to bed, his father gave him a
kiss. "Things might look better tomorrow," said Nick,
giving him an unsuccessful wink.

"Or the day after," Angus said. They looked at each
other and Angus was sure they were both thinking
the same thing. They were thinking: as long as it's not
because of the scarab.

It wasn't any better the next day. Nor the day after that. In fact, it got worse and worse. Angus went to school as usual, Nick thought that was the best thing to do. Two other children were ill, including Annalisa, luckily. Mr Scribble asked every day if Dummie was feeling better and Angus muttered, "not completely," and "it takes longer with him," and that sort of things. He was more occupied with Dummie than with the lessons, but Mr Scribble gave him some space. Maybe he thought Angus was coming down with it too. In the meantime, Angus kept searching the school for the scarab. But he'd looked in all the possible places three times by now. And no one was behaving suspiciously. No one had mentioned the scarab and no one had whispered or gone red when Mr Scribble asked after Dummie.

On Friday, Mr Scribble kept Angus back after school.

"Will you send my best to Dummie?" he asked. And when Angus looked worried: "Please don't worry. The competition isn't for another fortnight."

As though Angus was worrying about that!

On Saturday, Nick cycled into a ditch and broke his leg.

He'd chosen the worst time ever to cycle into a ditch and break his leg. It would have been stupid at any time, but Angus found this super-stupid. How could his father do this to him? He'd never had an accident in his life. Why did it have to happen now?

Nick had gone off to fetch break at half past eight in the morning and didn't return until half past twelve. In a taxi. No bread and his leg in plaster. He'd called at nine to say he'd been held up, and he hadn't even said why. That was because he didn't want to worry Angus, he told him afterwards.

But Angus had been terribly worried, and when he saw the taxi pulling up he'd rushed outside. As it emerged from the taxi, he'd looked at the plaster cast in astonishment. And it turned out to be attached to his father.

"What have you done?" he cried.

"Hang on," Nick groaned. He paid the taxi driver, struggled inside on his crutches, sat down, put up his leg on a chair and finally said that it had snapped in two.

Angus was furious. "How could you go and break your leg!" he shouted. "You're supposed to be looking after Dummie."

"It was because of that stupid Miss Frick!" Nick shouted back. "That flibbergibbet cycled in front of me on her bike and zigzagged all over the place! I was overtaking her and suddenly she swung to the left. I tried to avoid her, turned my handlebars, hit the ditch, my leg got stuck in the bike and crack. Such a flibbergibbet! She needs to see an optician. Or she needs stabilisers! She can't cycle! She didn't even look back when it happened. Maybe she didn't even notice. Bat-eyed flibbergibbet!"

He was furious, otherwise he wouldn't have said

flibbergibbet three times.

"Now what?" Angus asked.

"Now it hurts!"

"I don't mean that, I mean Dummie! Who's going to look after Dummie?"

"I can hop around. A bit. I'll make it up the stairs. Rather slowly, like an old man with a hernia. You'll have to help, though."

"Great! Fantastic!" Angus shouted angrily. He couldn't believe it. Dummie was ill and his father's leg had snapped in two. It was just too much bad luck.

Now he'd have to do everything on his own: he'd have to look after his father and Dummie. He poured his father a cup of tea, he fried an egg, and followed his father when he went to the toilet, just in case he fell and broke his other leg. In the meantime, he went up- and downstairs constantly. Dummie didn't need any food or drink, but Angus wanted to check as often as possible whether he was getting any better. But he wasn't. It seemed as though Dummie was getting sicker and sicker. When Angus went upstairs for what must have been the hundredth time, he sat down on his bed. Dummie stank and muttered something incomprehensible every once in a while.

This wasn't good, Angus thought, worried. And it was getting worse fast. Was it only six weeks ago that he'd seen Dummie for the first time? It seemed as though he'd always been there. And now... He couldn't just—

His eye fell on the small green book on the bedside table. Would that be the only thing they had left of

the
book

Dummie soon? A memento? A book full of unreadable hieroglyphics? With that picture of the stupid scarab...? "Idiot!" he suddenly shouted out loud. He could hit himself on the head! That little green book! There was a picture of the scarab in it! It might explain about the scarab! Or it might say something else useful. A medicine they could use. A clue. A... whatever. How could they have forgotten the book?

He grabbed it from the bedside table, ran downstairs and shoved it under his father's nose. "Look! We'd forgotten all about this! It might give us the solution," he cried excitedly.

"The solution? What to?" Nick asked sheepishly.

"Dummie! The reason he's sick!"

"Huh? Yes. No. Yes, maybe," Nick said. He must have taken some painkillers because he looked at the book drowsily and rubbed his chin in confusion. "But we can't read it," he said.

"We can't. But maybe someone else can. Don't you think? There must be people who can read this?"

"I don't know," his father said in a tired voice.

Thoughts raced around Angus' mind. When they'd just found the book all they'd done was check on the internet a couple of times and when they'd failed to

understand anything, they'd just put the book on
the bedside table, like a kind of souvenir. "Maybe Mr
Scribble can read it," he suggested. "Mr Scribble knows
everything about Egypt."

"Mr Scribble? Can he read hieroglyphics?"

"I don't know! Maybe. Or he might know someone else
who can. Mr Scribble might be able to help us. Dad,
we have to do something. Dummie is getting so sick...
Dad, wake up!"

His father tried to think. "Alright. Take the book to

Mr Scribble. Ask if he can translate it for us. But don't say anything about Dummie. We agreed about that."

"Not even in an emergency?"

"No. Just don't."

Angus got up. "Alright, I'm going," he said. He walked over to the cupboard and had just found Mr Scribble's address in the phone book when his father suddenly grabbed him by his shoulders from behind.

"You're right, Angus. And tell him it's urgent. Oh, how stupid of me not to think of that myself. And this stupid leg... Ouch!"

"I'm off," Angus said.

Angus jumped onto his bike and cycled to Mr Scribble's house.

Mr Scribble lived on the other side of Polderdam in a terraced house with high windows. Angus rang the bell and rocked impatiently on his toes. It seemed like an eternity before the door opened and his teacher appeared.

"Hey, Angus," Mr Scribble said in surprise. "Has something happened?"

Angus hadn't thought of an answer to this. He had planned to adopt an innocent expression and act like it was the most normal thing in the world to turn up with a book full of hieroglyphics.

He got the book out of his bag and gave it to the teacher. "No, I just came about this. Can you read it?"

he asked, as casually as he could.

"This little book? Well, come in first." Mr Scribble went into the sitting room, put on his glasses and opened the book. "Aha. These are hieroglyphics," he said. He turned the book over and looked at it from all sides. Then he peered at Angus over his glasses, amazed. "This is really very old, you know. How did you get it?"

"I— My father bought it at a flea market," Angus quickly lied. "And we want to know what it says. Can you read it to me?"

"Read it to you? Hieroglyphics?" Mr Scribble smiled. "I can't just read them out. First you have to decipher them. They take some puzzling over."

"But can you do that, de— decipher it? It's important."

"Is it for your project?" Mr Scribble asked.

"No. Well, yes actually. A bit. Mr Scribble, it's really important that my father and I know what's in it as soon as possible. Today if possible. Can you? Today? Perhaps?"

Angus was being too impatient, because Mr Scribble suddenly looked suspicious. He leaned back, put the tips of his fingers together and asked: "What's really going on?"

"What do you mean?" Angus asked. Blasting cackdingle, and now he was blushing too.

"You can't buy this kind of book at a flea market," Mr Scribble said sternly.

"Well, it was more of an antiques shop. Or maybe I've forgotten." Angus bit his lip. He was being even more stupid than his father when he rode into a ditch.

He was ruining everything.

Mr Scribble looked at him with raised eyebrows. He didn't believe a word of it. "Is it Dummie's perhaps?" he asked. "He already had that funny old scarab."

Angus became even redder.

"And why the hurry?" Mr Scribble asked.

Because otherwise Dummie might die, just hurry up! Angus wanted to shout. But he couldn't, of course. Or could he? Yes, why not? Dummie might die because he had come up with some idiotic story about an antiques shop. His father couldn't help Dummie and he couldn't either. Mr Scribble probably couldn't help him either, but just maybe he could. All of a sudden Angus wanted to tell him everything.

"Can you keep a secret?" he asked. "A very big secret. One that nobody can know?"

Mr Scribble raised his eyebrows even higher.

"Please? Do you promise?"

"Is it that important?"

"Yes. Even more important!" Angus said.

"Alright, calm down," Mr Scribble said. "I won't tell anybody."

"OK. Good," Angus sighed. "It's about Dummie..." And then he told him everything. About that strange evening when Dummie had suddenly been lying in his bed. That he and his father had been scared to death but that they'd decided that Dummie should stay, because what else could they do. And that the next day they'd read about the traffic accident with the mummies in the paper. That they'd washed him and sprayed him with toilet freshener. Angus even told him about the vacuum cleaner. And about Dummie's scarab, which he'd got from his father, who was probably a pharaoh. That they'd found the book later, in the ditch where the accident happened. And he told him that his father had thought that Dummie was getting bored and that after long consideration, he'd decided he should go to school. And that nobody, not even Mr Scribble himself, had seen that Dummie was a mummy, because they'd said he'd been burned. And that he'd been terrified when Dummie had shown everyone his scarab. And that Dummie had lifted up his flap, nearly making Annalisa faint, but that she'd still thought she'd seen burn wounds. But that Dummie's scarab had got lost now and Dummie had become ill and that he and his father thought it might be because of the scarab. "And maybe there's something in that book that might help," Angus concluded. "There's a drawing of the scarab. Only we can't read it. Maybe nobody can. It's the scarab of Mukatagara. Have you ever heard of it?"

He stopped talking at last. He must have been rattling on for at least ten minutes and Mr Scribble hadn't interrupted him once. He'd just stared at him, shaking his head in disbelief from time to time.

"It's not possible," he said once Angus had fallen silent.

"It is possible! The bandages. And the scarab.... Have you ever heard of Mukatagara?"

"So Dummie's a living mummy?" Mr Scribble asked. "No, it's really not possible."

"It is possible, because it's true!" Angus cried. "He

might die! I'm asking you whether you've ever heard of the scarab. Just tell me, yes or no?" He was almost shouting and bursting into tears at the same time.

Mr Scribble stood up and got his coat. "I'm coming to your house," he said.

"No. You have to decipher the book!" Angus cried.

"I want to see him first. Under the bandages, I mean."

"But my father said no one can see him! He said that if anyone sees him, they'll take him away! And then they'll stick needles in him and saw his skull open and..."

"Silence!" Mr Scribble said. "Your father is right about that. But I won't do that, will I? I just want to see him. And if it's true what you say—"

"It is true!"

"And if it's true, I'll help you. Come on."

And so Angus and Mr Scribble cycled side by side to Angus' house. Angus didn't even feel relieved. In fact he felt rotten. He had given away their secret. He had put Dummie in danger. His father would be furious with him. And Dummie might die.

When they arrived at the house, Nick was struggling around the garden with his crutches. He saw Mr Scribble and must have understood at once that Angus had told him everything. He didn't seem surprised, more relieved.

Mr Scribble parked his bike and Nick sent Angus upstairs. Dummie was tossing and turning in bed. Angus looked out of the window and saw his father and Mr Scribble talking. A little while later the stairs creaked and the door opened.

Nick and Mr Scribble both had serious expressions. Mr Scribble walked over to the bed and laid his hand cautiously on Dummie's shoulder. "So this is— this is—"

"An ill mummy," Nick said. He opened Dummie's flap and showed Mr Scribble his face. Mr Scribble was shocked. Angus was shocked as well, because Dummie's face seemed to have aged a thousand years in a week.

"Please?" Nick said.

"Please?" Angus whispered.

Mr Scribble must have stood next to the bed for a minute. He had to believe in something that wasn't possible and that obviously took some time. "Good. Alright. That's just how it is. Good. Good," he said at last. He turned around. "I'll start right away," he said. "But I can't promise anything." He went downstairs and left without saying anything else.

Angus and Nick sat in the sitting room waiting. It was silly of them because Mr, Scribble wouldn't be able to translate it that quickly. But they didn't know what else to do. After a while they decided to play chess, but neither of them really had the energy for it, and after a couple of games, they put the board away.

Time crawled at a snail's pace. Nick telephoned Mr Scribble and he said he hadn't got very far yet. They turned on the TV, but didn't really watch it. Angus fried some eggs, but neither of them were hungry. Nick called Mr Scribble again and hung up. Angus went upstairs a hundred times and paced the room a thousand times. "Why does time always go so slowly?" he cried impatiently.

"Because we're sitting and waiting," his father sighed. "Maybe you should read a book or something."

"NO!"

In the evening Nick called Mr Scribble another three times. "I'm not allowed to call anymore," he said after the third time. Well, there they were then.

Angus and his father went to bed at the same time. Angus turned on his bedside lamp and saw that Dummie's new bandages were turning brown. He stank so badly that Angus opened the window. He thought it meant that Dummie was rotting. But that sounded so awful he put it out of his mind. He didn't sleep a wink that night.

On Sunday, at around midday, the bell went. Angus rushed to the door. It was Ebbi with a bouquet of hand-picked flowers in his hand.

"Oh. Hi, Ebbi," Angus said, disappointed.

"I've come to visit the patient," Ebbi said, cheerfully. "How's Dummie?"

"Yeah. Fine," Angus said.

"Can I see him?"

"Erm, no," Angus said quickly. "Dummie isn't allowed visitors. Because of the risk of infection – of the burns wounds, the doctor said. I don't feel too good myself, to be honest. And we've got other guests. And my father has broken his leg."

"Really?" Ebbi said, in disbelief.

"Yes. Because of Miss Frick. So I'm quite busy. I'll give him these, alright?" He took the flowers from Ebbi's hand, closed the door and opened it again immediately. "I'm sorry, Ebbi," he added. "I'll explain it another time, but I really am busy. I'm cooking. Thanks for the flowers. Really."

"I can help, you know," Ebbi said. "I can cook fish too."

"Cook fish?"

"Yes. I can smell fish."

Angus gave him such a surprised look that Ebbi laughed.

"Alright. I'll be on my way. Give half of the flowers to your father. And say hi to Dummie from me. Tell him I miss him." He raised his nose and sniffed. "Hurry now, before it burns. Bye, see you tomorrow."

Angus closed the door and shuddered. The house smelled of fish. Not because there was a fish in the pan, but because Dummie was rotting. How much clearer did it have to be?

He went to the sitting room and sat at the window with his father. He looked at the shadows, disappearing here and growing larger there. He didn't know what else to do and at least that way he was sure that time was passing.

At the end of the afternoon, Mr Scribble finally appeared on his bike. He had bags under his eyes and looked awful.

Angus ran to the door and yanked it open. "Have you found out anything?" he blurted out.

Mr Scribble nodded and came in. "How's Dummie?" he asked.

"He's getting worse," Nick said. "I think—" He looked at Angus and stopped.

Angus knew exactly what his father wanted to say. And because he didn't say it, he said it himself. "We think Dummie's dying," he said. And when he said aloud what he'd been thinking for two days, he got very cold inside and he began to cry. Nick noticed and pulled Angus towards him. And then they almost fell, because Nick couldn't balance with his leg in plaster.

They sat down on the sofa and Mr Scribble opened his bag. He gave Angus and his father a serious look. "I've been working away at one section. I worked all night. I consulted all the books I could find. It's difficult. Very difficult. Almost impossible, these hieroglyphics."

"But you did manage?" Angus asked.

Mr Scribble removed the book from his bag and a pile of papers with crossed out sentences, arrows and scrawls, which Angus thought looked harder to decipher than the hieroglyphics. Then he began to explain. Angus and Nick hung on his every word, they were so desperate to hear.

"As far as I can make out, the book was written by someone called Hepsetsut," Mr Scribble began. "There are three short pieces in it, kind of chapters. The first chapter is about the scarab and there's a picture of it too. The scarab of Mukatagara was clearly an important possession in those times. It says that the pharaoh always wore it in his crown, like an amulet. The scarab brought the pharaoh luck, I think. The pharaoh's name isn't there so I couldn't look up more."

"Akhnetut," Angus and Nick said at the same time.

"Akhnetut?" Mr Scribble asked. "You could have told me that earlier."

Angus and Nick nodded.

"Well, alright. Then there are six signs in a row, I think that they are six names. The holy one, that's Darwishi, the large, that's Ur-atum, the righteous, that's Minkabh…"

Angus and his father looked at each other. "That's Dummie," they said at the same time. "We took the first six letters of his name," Nick said, with a guilty expression.

"Oh," Mr Scribble said. "Well, you could have told me that too. It took me hours to work it out." He looked at them accusingly.

"Yes, we should have," Nick muttered.

"And what else?" Angus asked, before they could get into a discussion about how stupid he and his father had been.

"Yes. Well. What else. In the second chapter there's something about a kind of fire. And something about that fire and the scarab. The fire will make it shine, or something like that. But I don't understand much of it. I think the fire comes from the sky."

"That's lightning," Angus and Nick said together.

"At least, that's what we think," Angus hurriedly added, when Mr Scribble gave them an amazed look for the third time. He and his father really were stupid, because they hadn't told Mr Scribble that Dummie had made a drawing of lightning hitting his scarab. Blasting cackdingle, this could have all been sorted out much quicker.

"And the third chapter?" Angus asked.

"I'll read out the third chapter," Mr Scribble picked up his papers and leafed through them. "Here. This is what I made of it: 'The powerful scarab of Mukatagara will lead, erm— so that would be Dummie — on his journey through the underworld. Nothing shall harm him. No fire shall consume him, no snake shall strangle him, no insect shall poison him. The scarab gives the power to be and to vanquish.' Or something like that, I'm not completely sure." Mr Scribble looked up.

"Does it really say that?" Angus asked, incredulously. He thought it was very badly deciphered. That kind of nonsense was useless to them!

"There's something else," Mr Scribble said. "I think that Hepsetsut put a curse on the scarab. In the last line, it says: 'This is what I pronounce about the scarab of Mukatagara.' That's to curse, this pronounciation, I think. 'The scarab and Darwishi make each other shine. It belongs only to Darwishi and to no other. Evil is he who breaks the bond, sees more gold than is good for him and the gold shall make their eyes shine. And the fire of the underworld will touch him in his soul. And he will be older than he cares.'" Mr Scribble let the pages drop. "Or something like that," he said again. "I can't make any more of it than that."

"What does it mean?" Angus asked, excitedly.

And then Mr Scribble said something terrible. He said, "I don't know. Evil means a thief, I think. And in any case, it doesn't turn out well for the thief. I guess."

"You guess?" Angus asked, upset.

"I'm sorry," Mr Scribble said.

"It's not possible!" Angus cried in desperation. "You need to think more. What does it mean if someone gets fire in their soul? That he's on fire? And if he sees more gold than is good for him? Do we need to look for someone who suddenly has a lot of gold?"

"That might be too literal," Mr Scribble said. "Fire. Heat. I don't know. Gold means riches. But 'more than he cares for' means trouble. I really have no idea what he means."

"Gold, fire, money, trouble. So the thief might get ill?" Angus tried.

"Maybe."

"But everyone is ill at the moment! And there's a flu bug going around!"

"Exactly," said Mr Scribble with a sigh.

"Does it say anything about what's going to happen to Dummie?" Nick asked.

"No. The scarab and Darwishi make each other shine. Maybe that means it gives life. But that's already happened. I don't think that Darwishi can survive without the scarab. He might have a couple more weeks. Maybe just a few days. I don't know."

"Can't survive without it? So I was right? Is Dummie dying?" Angus cried.

Mr Scribble didn't reply. Of course, he didn't know the answer. But Angus felt desperate and angry at the same time. Mr Scribble always knew everything, why didn't he know this? He should try harder!

Nick got up. "Thanks anyway," he said.

"I want to pop up and see him again," Mr Scribble said, looking exhausted.

They went upstairs. It did stink of fish, Angus thought. A whole bucket of rotten cod.

Dummie lay slackly in bed. "Dad, weren't his eyes gold?" Angus whispered.

Nick looked at Dummie's eyes. "Yes. But they aren't anymore," he said.

Mr Scribble went home, but he said he'd keep looking for anything about Hepsetsut, the pharaoh called Akhnetut and the scarab of Mukatagara.

It was only eight o'clock, but Nick said that Angus should go to bed because he had school again in the morning.

"I'm not going to school!" Angus shouted. "How can I go to school if Dummie might be dying? We have to look for the scarab. I have to find the thief. I have to—"

"You have to sleep," Nick said. "And so do I."

They went to bed. Angus' bedroom smelled like a fish stall in the summer, but Angus couldn't even smell it. He got into bed and listened to Dummie's rattling breathing. He wracked his brains. He thought so hard his head hurt. Or maybe it was because of the stench, he wasn't sure. He had to go through all the points, like his father always did. Fire. Gold. Sickness. Should they go to all the hospitals and find out who'd suddenly fallen ill? Should they look for a pyromaniac? Or a jeweller? Gold would make his eyes shine. Dummie's eyes shone because they were made of gold. Would the thief get golden eyes? A normal person wouldn't see anything with gold eyes. Should they look up people who had suddenly gone blind?

A different line of thinking then. About evil. If the scarab was stolen, was evil the thief? Which people had seen the scarab? Everyone in the class. So if there was a thief, it was someone at school. Angus only needed to look. How was he going to go about it? Interrogate all of the children? That would take much too long! But he couldn't just stand up in class and ask who'd stolen Dummie's scarab. The thief would never admit it. At the most they might get nervous. Turn red. Start to sweat— Whaah! Angus felt like shouting. That was it! The solution! A thief would get nervous! And more so if he went about it creatively. Blasting cackdingle! He should ask it. Not in a direct way, but differently. He would lie and bluff, just like his father. He would tell the class that Dummie's scarab had been stolen and that his father had gone to the police. And that the police had come round yesterday and said they'd almost caught the thief. The real thief would panic about that, wouldn't they? He'd spin a good story and have a good look to see who got nervous. Angus turned, thought some more and suddenly found it a stupid idea. But a stupid idea was better than no idea.

And Dummie was dying...

CHAPTER 7

Who's the Thief?

The next morning Angus got up early. "I am going to school," he said. He told his father about his plan. "Do you think it will work, Dad? That they'll get nervous?"

"Ever since Dummie turned up, anything's been possible," Nick said darkly. He had slept as badly as Angus because his leg had itched all night, as though a herd of ants were marching along under the plaster, he said.

"Dad! Don't you think it's a good idea?"

"My idea is to tell everything to the police. I mean everything. Then the police will have to look. They are much better at that."

"But then everything will come out!" Angus cried. "Shouldn't I try this first? As a last attempt? Dad?"

Nick nodded. "Fine. As a last attempt," he said.

At eight o'clock Nick cycled to school. If this didn't work, his father would go to the police. Perhaps they should have done that right away. They understood thieves and Dummie wouldn't be lying there like that now. But then the secret would have been out, and if those horrible scientists had taken Dummie away afterwards, he would be in an even worse state.

Angus parked his bike and went to his classroom. Mr Scribble was already there. He still looked tired. "How's Dummie?" he asked in concern.

Angus quickly explained his plan. "Would you ask how Dummie is?" he said. "And can you help me look? For the one who gets nervous? If it doesn't work, my father's going to the police."

Mr Scribble promised. And before starting the lesson, he stood in the middle of the classroom and asked how Dummie was.

Angus took a deep breath. "Dummie is still ill," he said. "Flu. Did I mention already that his scarab is missing?"

"The gold one?" Mr Scribble asked in feigned shock. Angus had a good look around him. "At first we thought he'd lost it," he said. "But then we went to the police anyway and they came round yesterday with some good news." Angus didn't know that he was such a good liar, the words just flowed out. He carried on with his story and kept a sharp look out. "The police said that they were on the trail of the thief. The person responsible will probably be arrested today. And because it's such a valuable object, the thief will probably get a long sentence, they said."

"Oh," Lizzy said, shocked. She clapped her hand to her mouth and blushed. Angus saw it at once. Lizzy was bright red! She wriggled in her chair as thought it was covered in itching powder, and stared at him anxiously. Angus felt like jumping for joy. Lizzy! Annalisa's friend. And Annalisa was ill! Annalisa had the scarab! He was sure of it!

"Well, the thief deserves their punishment," Mr Scribble said. "Do tell Dummie I hope he gets better soon."

Then the lesson started. Angus found it hard to work and kept looking at Lizzy. She sat there the whole time wriggling in her seat with a face like a tomato and didn't seem to be able to concentrate either.

When the bell went for break time, Angus got up. "It's Lizzy," he whispered to Mr Scribble. Lizzy hurried outside, but Angus ran quickly after her, overtook her and blocked her path. "Are you in a hurry?" he asked.

Lizzy looked at the floor.

"I didn't mention everything by the way, about the scarab," Angus said. "The officers were from the youth department. They're coming to the school this afternoon. They asked me to tell the class. Maybe someone will regret it. And children don't get punished as much if they confess to the police. They asked whether Dummie had any enemies. So I told them that the two of you had bullied him a lot."

He'd done brilliantly. Lizzy opened up at once. "I didn't take the scarab," she whimpered. "Annalisa had it. We found it on Monday after gym, under the climbing frame, in the sand. Annalisa took it. Dummie is a nasty show-off, with that gold thing. We wanted to punish him. He's a disgusting little boy."

"A disgusting little boy?" Angus felt a fit of rage swell up inside. He wanted to swear at Lizzy. Hit her. Tear her to pieces. He grabbed her hard. "And where is it now?" he screamed.

"I-I don't know," Lizzy stammered. "I haven't seen Annalisa all week. She's ill." Then the stupid girl began to cry. "Will Annalisa go to prison?"

"Yes! And you will too! Because you knew about it!

That counts too!" Angus shouted viciously. "Stupid, stupid— Cow!" He turned around, returned to the classroom and told Mr Scribble that Annalisa had the scarab. "I'm going to see her," he said. "Just tell the class I've come down with flu. I'm off."

Mr Scribble laid a hand on his shoulder. "Well done, Angus. Hurry. I'll come round to your house straight from school."

Angus got on his bike and cycled as fast as he could to Annalisa's house.

Annalisa lived in a large detached house on the edge of the village. On the way, Angus thought about what he was going to say. He was coming to visit her because she was ill. Without a present? He'd come to drop off some homework. In the middle of the day? Blasting cackdingle. He couldn't think straight. All he really wanted to do was give Annalisa a good thrashing. He didn't usually think things like that, but now he did. Maybe it was because of Dummie. Dummie had wanted to hit Annalisa the whole time. And it might have worked better too. If Dummie had hit her, she might not have dared steal his scarab. How ill was she? Seriously ill? Things didn't turn out well for the thief, Mr Scribble had said. But how bad was not well?

Mrs Stickler opened the door. Luckily she didn't recognise him. If she'd known that Dummie lived with him, she probably would have slammed the door in his face. Now she put her hands in her sides and gave

Angus a questioning look.

"I've brought some homework for Annalisa," Angus said, as innocently as he could.

"Lizzy is supposed to bring it," Mrs Stickler snapped.

"Lizzy couldn't come this afternoon," Angus said.

"Then no homework. This is the mayor's house and I can't just let anyone in. Anyway, children with flu don't have to do homework."

"But I have a special assignment, for the schools' competition," Angus lied. "The teacher sent me. It's really important. You know..." He was standing there, wracking his brains for what else to say when a phone rang somewhere. Mrs Stickler hesitated. "Well, five minutes then. Upstairs, first door on the left," she said. She turned around and Angus ran upstairs.

Annalisa was lying in bed under a pink duvet. There was a half-full glass of orange juice on the bedside table. When she saw Angus, she seemed more surprised than scared. Angus looked at her eyes. They weren't gold. "Where's the scarab?" he asked bluntly.

"Which scarab?" she asked with a hoarse voice.

"Dummie's scarab of course! You stole it! And don't play the innocent, Lizzy told me herself."

Annalisa said nothing. Angus couldn't see whether she'd gone red or not because her face already looked like a tomato. He walked over to her and balled his fists. It wouldn't take much for him to actually hit her. "I'll go to the police if you don't tell me where it is," he threatened.

Now Annalisa looked scared. But she still didn't say anything.

"Where's the scarab?!" Angus screamed in anger.
"Tell me! Where? If you don't tell me where it is, I'll—"
He raised his fist.

Annalisa began to scream.

Fast footsteps came running up the stairs and
Mrs Stickler entered with the telephone in her hand.
"What's going on?" she snarled.

"Annalisa stole Dummie's scarab! I'm going to the
police and she's going to prison!"

Mrs Stickler gave him an astonished look. Then she

became just as angry. "My daughter doesn't steal!" she cried.

"She does! Lizzy told me. She stole the scarab and that's why she got sick. I need it back. Now! If she gives it back, she'll get better!"

It sounded ridiculous, of course. Mrs Stickler thought so too. "Leave now, or I'll call the police!" she shouted. She grabbed Angus by the arm and dragged him into the corridor. Angus stumbled and almost fell down the stairs. But he wasn't going to let her send him away! He turned around, stormed back into the bedroom, seized Annalisa by the shoulders and shook her. "Tell me!" he raged. "Now! Or I'll set Dummie on you! Tell me!"

And then Annalisa told him. "I don't have it anymore," she whispered.

"What?

"I just found it by the climbing frame. It was in the sand. I picked it up."

"And then what? Where is it now?"

"In Miss Frick's goldfish bowl. Because Dummie's frightened of water."

"In the goldfish bowl?" Angus shrieked. He was bursting with anger. The stupid girl had only gone and thrown Dummie's scrarab in a goldfish bowl! "Do you have any idea what you have done?"

"Annalisa, dear. What have you—?" Mrs Stickler was standing next to them.

Angus pushed the ugly lady aside, ran downstairs and out of the house.

Angus cycled back to school as fast as he could. His blood was boiling. What had he expected? That she'd be wearing it around her neck? That she'd have golden eyes? The girl just had flu. But she had taken the scarab and now Angus knew where it was. In five minutes he'd be fishing it out of the goldfish bowl. And then back home and then....

Panting, Angus threw his bike against the bike rack and sprinted into the school. He ran straight to Miss Frick's office and yanked at her door. It was locked. Locked? Angus ran back outside and round the building to the window. It was closed. Closed! Angus pressed his nose against the glass and saw the goldfish bowl on her desk. There, less than three metres away, was Dummie's scarab. But how was he going to get to it? Did Mr Scribble have a key perhaps?

He ran back into the school, but his classroom was empty. Gym. They had gym. He had to go to the gymnasium. He ran back out and ran smack bang into someone. "Hey, Angus," a voice said.

Angus looked into the surprised face of Miss Paula.

"What's going on? Have you lost your classmates?" the first year teacher asked.

"No, my gym shorts," Angus lied. "I have to find them. I'm ill and am going home. I think they're in Lost Property, in the box in Miss Frick's office. My father wants to wash them. He's broken his leg. I need them. I—I—" This was ridiculous, he was acting like a headless chicken. "Do you have a key to her office? Please? Why isn't she there? Please?"

Miss Paula smiled. "Calm down," she said. "Miss

Frick has got flu. She's been off for a couple of days already. And you seem to have it too. You just need to go home. I'll lend you the key for a moment. Get your shorts and hurry home to bed." She stroked Angus' hair as though he was one of her first years. Angus smiled back foolishly, he could have kissed her.

Less then a minute later he was standing in front of Miss Frick's door with the key. It was a while before his shaking fingers got it into the slot and then he was facing the goldfish bowl. Angus looked in disgust at the slimy, green sediment. It stank and two dead goldfish floated upside down in the water. Was Dummie's scarab in there?

Without hesitating, he put his hand into the water

and felt around. Gravel. Miss Frick was ill. Slippery plants. A couple of days already. Another dead fish. Bat-eyed flibbergibbet, his father had said. No scarab. There was something wrong with her eyes. No scarab! Because she had it! Angus pulled his hand back out of the slime and almost shouted. Blasting cackdingle! He'd almost found it and now it had gone again! He wiped his hands on his trousers, locked the door again, gave the key to a small child in the corridor and stormed out of the school.

For the third time that day he jumped on his bike. He had no idea where Miss Frick lived, so he raced home. Nick was in the sitting room and jumped out of his skin when he saw Angus. He probably looked like he'd seen all the ghosts in the world. Angus breathlessly explained about Lizzy, Annalisa and the goldfish bowl, and then his father started to look peculiar, he was so angry. Angus and Nick looked up Miss Frick's address in the phone book. She lived quite close by.

"I'm off!" Angus cried.

"You can't go alone," Nick forbade. "If she really does have the scarab—"

"Then I'll get it from her and come back. And you need to look after Dummie. How's he doing?"

"Even worse. I'll call Mr Scribble."

"He won't be done until three o'clock. I'm not waiting for that. I'm going now!" And without listening to his father, Angus tore up the garden.

Ten minutes later, he stood panting before the door of a small, grey house. He took a deep breath and studied the name plate under the bell. "L. Frick" it said. Leonora Frick. So this was where she lived. Angus hoped that she was desperately ill. That worms were coming out of her ears. He hoped she was crazy sick. But not so crazy sick that she wouldn't be able to tell him where Dummie's scarab was.

Angus rang the bell.

Nothing.

He rang again. And then again for a long time.

He started to sweat. She might be dead. Things wouldn't turn out well for her. Turn out? End up? Dead? No, that wasn't possible, was it? Angus ran around the outside of the house and looked up. There was a balcony above him. And the balcony door was on the latch.

Angus didn't think twice, he put a garden chair under the balcony and heaved himself up the rain pipe. His arms weren't usually strong enough to do that but they seemed to be today. He pulled and lifted himself and then he was on the balcony. He peered inside and saw a bed. There was a motionless figure lying on it. Was she already—?

Angus unhooked the latch with shaking fingers, went inside and walked over to the bed. Full of disgust, he stared down at, erm— Miss Frick? It must be her because of the jam jar glasses on her nose. But the rest of her was unrecognisable. Her skin had turned brown. There were cracks in it and her nose seemed to be hanging off. Her whole face had shrivelled up and her mouth gaped open. There were a few flies hovering around her head. To Angus' horror, one even crawled out of her ear. Angus thought about Dummie's brown face. Would she become just like Dummie? Was Miss Frick turning into a mummy?

She must have heard him, because suddenly her eyes shot open. Angus clapped his hand to his mouth in fear. Dummie's eyes were looking out at him, eyes of pure gold. More gold than is good for you, shot through his mind. Older than you'd care. If he had any doubt about that, it had gone now. Miss Frick clearly didn't have flu. She had the scarab!

"Who's there?" Miss Frick called out. Her scratchy voice was almost incomprehensible. "Are you there again? Go away, I said!" She slapped her hands to her face and began to make a horrid sort of noise, halfway between sobbing and screaming. "No! No! Leave me alone!"

Angus looked around the room. She could see something. Or someone. But there wasn't anybody there.

All of a sudden Miss Frick sat up, threw a pair of scaly legs over the edge of the bed and stood up. She stank of rotting eel and looked awful. Older than she cared. As old as a mummy— She tottered to the door, her arms outstretched, the flies keeping pace with her. "I did it!" she muttered. "I don't have it anymore. How was I supposed to know? Leave me alone!"

Fire in her soul, Angus thought. Could she see

ghosts? Alright! Then he was the ghost! "Where's the scarab?" he roared. "Where?"

"Go away! I did it'

Angus pushed her back onto the bed, bent over her and grabbed her by the throat. Her skin tore, but he didn't care. "What did you do? Where is it? Tell me! Where's the scarab?"

Miss Frick rolled her head. Her golden eyes couldn't see. And then she muttered something terrible. She said, "I found it. But I can't find the boy. I can't see him! I can't give it back! But I don't have it anymore. It's over!"

"Where is it?"

"Gone. Thrown away!"

"Thrown away? Where?" Angus shouted, out of his mind with rage.

"R-rubbish bin," she said, "Outside."

"The big brown one?"

Angus rushed to a room on the front of the house and looked out of the window. There it was. On the street with its lid open. As he stood there watching, someone came out of the house next door and rolled Miss Frick's bin into her garden. It was like someone had slapped Angus in the face.

The rubbish bin. It was Monday morning. The bin men came to empty the bins on Monday mornings.

"Stupid idiot! We'll never find it now!" he yelled.

The Grobbe Museum

CHAPTER 8

A Close Shave

Then Angus really started to despair. He ran downstairs without giving Miss Frick another glance and went outside. As he cycled home, his mind reeled. He had caught the thief. But he'd been too late. That was the curse. Someone or something had taken revenge on him. Miss Frick was seeing ghosts and she'd shrivelled up. Or something like that, he didn't understand it entirely, no one could understand a thing like that, it was just too gruesome. At the back of Angus' mind a voice was screaming. *Help her! She doesn't deserve this. No one deserves that!* "No!" Angus cried. "But she didn't even steal it, she only found it in the fishbowl. She should have given it back and deserves to be punished for that. But punished like that? It's all because of the scarab!" The scarab! The voice was right. That thing was highly dangerous. But it had brought Dummie back to life. Without the scarab, Dummie would have been dead. They'd have to bury Dummie soon. Because of Miss Frick! He wasn't going to help anyone who'd thrown a thing like that in the bin. You couldn't trust anyone! Not Annalisa, because she'd thrown it in the water. Not Miss Frick, because she'd taken the scarab home and not Mr Scribble because he was supposed to know everything, only he didn't know how to make Dummie better. And not his father, because he had to go and break his leg, and he certainly couldn't trust himself either. Because he'd messed everything up.

Nick was sitting in the garden with his leg up. Mr Scribble was there too. Nick had called him at school and he'd immediately signed off sick. He was still holding his bike and gesturing frantically. When he saw Angus, he ran over to him.

"And?" he cried.

"No. She doesn't have it anymore!"

Angus cried as he told them what he'd seen. That Miss Frick had gone mad. That she looked like she was half mummy. And that the scarab of Mutakatagara was somewhere at the rubbish dump, amongst the gnawed off chicken bones and empty milk cartons. "Can't we go and look for it there?" he sobbed.

His father shook his head. "It all ends up in a big heap, son."

And when Mr Scribble added that they actually burned the rubbish nowadays, Angus started to feel sick with misery. "Dad, you need to call the doctor," he whispered.

"The doctor can't do anything for Dummie."

"For Miss Frick, I mean. You have to! She's helpless. They'll find her otherwise. And then they'll saw open her head."

Angus kept going on about it until Mr Scribble ended up leaving for Miss Frick's house and Angus stayed with his father. Nick hobbled up the stairs after Angus.

Dummie was lying in bed without moving. He didn't make a sound anymore. Angus looked at the pitiful pile of bandages and wished that Dummie had never turned up.

The afternoon passed by slowly. In the evening, Mr Scribble returned from Miss Frick's. He said that he hadn't climbed in through the balcony but had borrowed the spare key from the neighbour. He'd spent the afternoon at her bedside and her skin had become a little less brown. He thought she was getting a little bit better because she no longer had the scarab. He had kept the key to her house and would go and check on her again the next day.

Angus and Nick spent the rest of the evening sitting with Dummie.

Monday became Tuesday and Mr Scribble came again and the three of them sat next to Dummie's bed. They were all sitting there waiting for Dummie to die.

It was terrible.

Then it was Wednesday. Angus had hardly slept and he and his father were sitting at the table staring at their toast. The phone rang. And again. When it rang for the third time, Angus picked it up. He said, "We're not at home," and hung up again. After that they just let the phone ring until it stopped on its own.

Ten minutes later, Mr Scribble cycled up the garden path. He threw his bike against the wall and waved a newspaper excitedly.

"The paper," Nick muttered. "What do we care about the news right now?"

Angus opened the door and Mr Scribble shoved the paper into his hands. "Page seven!" he panted. "The scarab."

Suddenly Angus was alert. He hurriedly leafed through the paper. Page three. Five. Seven.

He could hardly believe his eyes. There it was:

UNLUCKY MUSEUM FINDS GOLDEN SCARAB

Under the headline was a large picture of the scarab. There was no doubt about it. It was the scarab of Mukatagara.

"Whumpy dumpman!" Nick cried.

"Blasting cackdingle!" Angus cried.

They raced through the article. It turned out that the scarab had been found at the rubbish processing plant. That's where they extract metal from the rubbish with giant magnets. So the iron chain on the scarab had saved them! An attentive employee had seen the scarab shining and had been honest enough to hand it over to his boss. He had been just as honest and had taken the scarab to The Grobbe Museum, which had recently suffered some bad luck when three mummies had been destroyed while being delivered. The scarab was now on display in the Egyptian room.

"It really is the scarab," Angus whispered.

"It's back!" Nick cried.

Then Angus, Nick and Mr Scribble all looked at each other. They were all thinking the same thing. A museum. Guards. How on earth were they going to get hold of the thing?

"We'll just go and get it," Angus said. "It is ours. It's lost property, isn't it, Dad?"

"And how did we get it?" his father asked. "What do we say then? That we got it from a mummy?"

"Don't be stupid!" Angus cried. "It's just ours. We need it!"

Angus saw his father and Mr Scribble looking at each other. "Then I'm going to steal it," he said. "I really will. You can't stop me. I'm going to steal it, otherwise Dummie will die!"

"How is Dummie?" Mr Scribble asked.

"Not long left," Nick said.

"Shut up about Dummie! Think about how you can help me. I'm going to steal it! And if you don't help, I'll do it on my own!"

Nick and Mr Scribble looked at each other again. "Don't worry. I'll help you," Mr Scribble said.

Now they knew where the scarab was, Angus felt hopeful again. His father, Mr Scribble and Angus tried to come up with a plan. Maybe all three of them were too honest because they couldn't think of a good one. Mr Scribble looked at his watch. "The museum opens at ten o'clock," he said. "Let's just go and have a look at it. Maybe we'll have an idea when we see how the scarab is displayed."

Nick stayed home with Dummie and Angus and Mr Scribble got into Nick's car.

It was a half hour's drive and Angus frowned and fretted all the way. Maybe the scarab was in a glass case with glass so hard you could only break it with a baseball bat. But you could hardly take a baseball bat into a museum. Or maybe there was a guard next to it. Would they have to knock him out? Maybe they should set fire to something? Cause a bomb scare? Break in at night? Hire a thief?

Mr Scribble parked, they hurried to the desk and bought two tickets. Then it took them at least ten minutes to find the right room. Finally they spotted it:

the scarab of Mukatagara was in the middle of a room on a cushion under a glass dome. Angus' stomach hurt. Right in front of him was the very dangerous

guard

← the scarab

object that could save Dummie. Wonderful. And terrible. Because how were they ever going to get hold of the scarab? In the corner of the room was a guard sitting on a chair. He stood up threateningly every time anyone got too close to something.

"Now what?" Angus whispered. "Any ideas?"

"We need to get rid of the guard, in any case," Mr Scribble said in a hushed voice. "But even then— the scarab is in the middle of the room. If we could get it, and I mean if, it's absence would be obvious at once. We wouldn't even get as far as the door."

As they walked around pretending to study everything carefully, Angus thought so hard his brains creaked. Mr Scribble was right: maybe they could steal it. One of them should distract the guard and the other one get the scarab. That's how they did it in films. But they'd all see the scarab was missing right away. It was simply impossible....

And then, in a flash, Angus had an idea. He didn't know where it came from but it was an excellent idea. He hurried over to Mr Scribble who was staring at an empty wall, sunk in thought. "I've thought of something," he said. "What if you had a heart attack? You're old. That wouldn't be so strange?"

"Sorry? A heart attack?"

"Not a real one, just pretend. Fall down."

"Then what?"

Angus explained his plan.

Mr Scribble gaped at him. "If that worked—" he said. And then excitedly, "Of course it will work! It's a fantastic idea. Come along. We need to tell your Dad!"

They found Nick at Dummie's bedside.

"Well?" he asked. Angus saw that he was giving Dummie an anxious look. Dummie was lying there like a flat balloon.

Mr Scribble shook his head. "It's the right scarab, it's lying there in a glass case in the middle of the room. But we've got a plan. Angus has a plan."

"It's too late. I think Dummie will— Today—" Nick said.

"It's not too late!" Angus shrieked. "You need to act. Now. You're supposed to be an artist. Can't you make something? Out of clay?"

"Clay?" his father repeated foolishly.

"Wake up, Dad!" Angus shouted. "You need to mould a scarab out of clay! A fake one. Then I'll go back with Mr Scribble and Mr Scribble will have a heart attack and I'll snatch the scarab and put the other one in its place!" He'd never shouted at his father like that before, but he had to. His father was just sitting there like a saggy pudding. Angus shook his shoulder frantically.

"Which other one?" Nick asked.

"The one you're going to make! Think, Dad! I'll swap them! No one will notice then. You can make one, can't you? I've still got some of that fast-drying stuff. Hurry and do it! Now!"

Nick finally came to his senses. He shook his head and stood up. "Alright. Sorry. Yes. No. I don't know if it will work. But I'll do it. I'll go and make one straight away."

And he did just that. Mr Scribble gave him the

green book with the picture of the scarab and Nick set to work. Angus sat beside him and watched as his fathers kneaded and shaped the clay. Slowly a scarab emerged. His father was a better artist than Angus thought. The scarab looked just like the real thing. Once this was all over, maybe his father should turn his hand to sculpture.

Nick pricked the scarab on a stick and showed it to Mr Scribble who was sitting with Dummie. When he said the scarab was very good, Nick put it on the windowsill.

After half an hour, the fake scarab was dry. Nick got a spray can of gold paint from the shelf and a small brush, and carefully painted the scarab gold.

While the paint dried, they all sat with Dummie. Angus looked at his horrifying face. His skin was full of cracks and there was brown sludge oozing from his mouth.

"Hang on in there," he whispered at Dummie's face. "We're getting your scarab. Hang on in there. MAASHI? Don't give up."

They went through the plan again. Angus and Mr Scribble would take a taxi. Mr Scribble would have a heart attack and Angus would swap the scarabs. Nick thought they should have a fall-back plan for if it went wrong. "What if you get caught? How will you get out of that?"

"Then I'm just a thief," Angus said. "I did it for the schools' competition or something like that. You'll make a lot of noise, won't you? So that everyone looks at you? You have to act like you're dying." Then he did an impression. "Whaah! Aargh! That's what I mean. Then no one will pay any attention to me. Right? Can you do that?"

"Yes, I'll manage," Mr Scribble said. "Whaah! Aaargh!"

They were very serious and yet acting like lunatics, next to Dummie's bed.

"And if they take Mr Scribble to hospital? How will you get home?" Nick asked.

"With another taxi, I suppose," Angus said.

"Do you dare to do that on your own?"

"If I've just stolen a scarab, I won't be afraid of getting a taxi, will I?"

"OK. A taxi." Nick sighed and gave a Angus a purse full of money. He wrapped up the fake scarab in a paper bag and gave it to Angus, who carefully put it in his pocket. Then he picked up the phone and called a taxi.

"I wish I could do it myself," he said, after he'd hung up. "That bat-eyed freak has gotten us into a right mess."

Miss Frick. Angus had forgotten all about her. Was she still lying in her bedroom?

Mr Scribble shook his head. "Dummie already put you in a tight spot by coming here in the first place. And you've gotten yourselves into a mess by letting him stay."

"Yes, but listen. What else were we supposed to do?"

"Nothing. I think I would have done the same," Mr Scribble said. He looked at the clock. "Shall we go and wait outside?" he said.

The taxi arrived and Angus and Mr Scribble set off for the museum for the second time that day. The lady at the desk recognised them and they were allowed to use the same tickets again. Silently, they made their way to the Egyptian room.

There were three people in the room. Mr Scribble didn't think that was enough. No people meant no confusion, he said. Angus thought it was better that way: the fewer people, the better, but Mr Scribble thought they should wait. By now, Angus was stiff with nerves. They walked around the glass dome, looked at an empty sarcophagus and even looked at the next room. There were a few paintings with just blobs on them and it occurred to Angus that even his father could do better. Not long afterwards, they saw a group of elderly people go into the Egyptian room and they hurried after them. Angus' heart was racing as though he was sprinting. Maybe one of the old people would have a heart attack, that would be good. He shouldn't think that, of course, but it would be handy.

Angus and Mr Scribble pretended to be interested in everything in the room all over again. Angus couldn't see a thing by now, he was too nervous to look. His hand gripped the clay scarab in his pocket. His father had added an iron chain to it and it looked exactly like the real scarab.

Angus and Mr Scribble went over to the dome and looked at Dummie's scarab. Suddenly Angus felt warm. What if it was fixed down? They wouldn't leave such a valuable thing unattached, would they? And no one could just lift a glass dome in a museum. That would be much too easy for a thief. No, that thing was probably completely stuck down. He began to sweat.

Mr Scribble nudged him and nodded.

"Wait a sec," Angus whispered in near panic.

"No, now," Mr Scribble said and walked a few paces away. Angus panicked. It wouldn't work. It was a crazy idea. Everyone would see him. Who had come up with this stupid plan anyway?

"Whaah! Aargh!" Mr Scribble moaned. He rolled his eyeballs and sank to the floor as though his legs were suddenly made of jelly.

A few people looked up. Not much happened really. No one reacted, in any case.

"Hey! My uncle's having a heart attack!" Angus cried out. "Help him! Who can do mouth-to-mouth?"

"Whaaah! Aargh!"

"Don't just stand there watching! Do something!"

Finally the people rushed towards Mr Scribble, who was lying on the floor, groaning even louder. Angus thought that someone whose heart wasn't working wouldn't be able to make so much noise. But it did work. Angus slipped out of the circle and looked around nervously. No one was looking at him, even the guard was standing over Mr Scribble. He had to do it now. But he didn't dare! Yes, he did! He must! No! Yes! Do it!

Angus ran to the dome, looked around again and then laid his hands on it.

Please let it not be fixed down, he thought. Let me lift it...

And then he did it.

The dome was loose. But it was alarmed! A sound like a foghorn blared out through the room. Angus jumped out of his skin. He let go of the dome and on an impulse pushed the whole base over.

The dome rolled away and the scarab of Mukatagara rolled across the floor. Angus dived after it, grabbed it, felt in his pocket and swapped it with the other. To his horror, the two chains got tangled up and were stuck for a moment. Blasting cackdingle! He tugged them apart in despair. But now he no longer knew which was which! He picked one at random and put it in his pocket. At the same time he was grabbed roughly from behind. "What are you doing?"

"I'm sorry! It was an accident!" Angus cried. "I

tripped! That's my uncle! My favourite uncle's having a heart attack."

"Where's the scarab?" the guard snarled.

"Here. I picked it up for you. It was on the floor. Here it is. I'm sorry. How's my uncle?"

The guard fell for it. He let go of Angus and took the scarab. As Angus ran to Mr Scribble, the guard put everything back in its place and turned off the alarm at last.

"Uncle Scribble! Uncle Scribble!" Angus called.

Mr Scribble opened his eyes. "It's passing now, kid," he muttered. He went to get up but other people held him down. The only thing Angus could do was to sit down next to Mr Scribble. The scarab was burning a hole in his pocket. Five minutes later, two men turned up with a stretcher. Someone must have called the emergency services.

Mr Scribble leaned back and closed his eyes again.

"Uncle Scribble," Angus cried again and bent down over him.

"Have you got it?" Mr Scribble whispered in his ear.

"I think so," Angus whispered back.

Then he was pulled aside and Mr Scribble was checked out by the two medics.

Angus looked around. No one was paying any attention to him. Now was the time to go.

The scarab held tightly in his hand, Angus left the museum. He acted as normal as possible. He didn't run and he looked straight ahead. But his heart was pounding again. What if he had taken the wrong one? That couldn't be possible, could it? What if he had taken the wrong one?

There was a taxi rank in front of the museum. Angus tapped on a window and gave his address.

"Do you have any money?" the man asked.

"I wouldn't ask otherwise, would I?" Angus said.

"You can never be sure," the man said.

Angus showed him his money and then he was allowed to sit up front. Angus didn't want to sit in the front seat, he wanted to look at the scarab. To make matters worse, the driver launched into a long story. Angus didn't even hear what it was about. He said yes or no from time to time, just guessing when. He let his fingers slide over the scarab. Rock hard. He tried to scratch it with his fingernails. He withdrew his hand and looked at his nails. No gold paint. It must be the right one!

"Dad! Dad!" Angus cried as he went inside. He ran into the sitting room. Nobody. He turned around and ran upstairs.

"Dad!" He stopped halfway up the stairs. It felt like someone was running an icy hand over his back. It was quiet in the house. Much too quiet. Dead silent. He couldn't—?

Angus stormed up the last steps and flew into his bedroom.

Nick was sitting on the bed with Dummie on his lap. Dummie's eyes were closed and his bandages were dripping with brown slime.

Angus' heart almost stopped. "Is he dead?" he cried.

Nick shook his head. "Shhh," he whispered. And then, "Have you got it?"

Angus pulled the scarab out of his pocket and hung it around Dummie's neck. He pushed the scarab carefully between the bandages until it was no longer visible. Now it was where it belonged. And Angus felt terrible.

He sat down next to his father and Dummie and Nick put his arm around him. He slowly rocked Angus and Dummie backwards and forth. Then he began to softly hum the Egyptian song that Dummie had taught them. Angus slowly began to unwind. He felt himself become slack. And then he began to cry. He cried and cried until his shoulders shook and he collapsed in a heap. "Dummie, wake up," he sobbed. "Wake up. Please, Dad..."

They must have sat on Dummie's bed for an hour. Nick humming from time to time and Angus crying.

After an hour, Nick lay Dummie down gently on his back. Angus couldn't take his eyes from Dummie's face. That ugly face, which he'd had to get used to and which he was afraid he was now looking at for the last time. His eyes filled up with tears again.

"Look," Nick whispered.

Angus quickly blinked away his tears.

"His eyes, Angus, look."

Angus bent over him and looked. Dummie's ugly eyelashes were fluttering. They opened a fraction for a second and Angus saw a glimmer of gold.

"Did you see that?" his father whispered.

"Yes," Angus whispered. "I can see it. I can really see it." And he couldn't stop himself from crying again anyway.

It was already late afternoon when Dummie carefully sat up and tried to perch on the edge of his bed. He only just managed it and then lay back down again, but Angus was over the moon. Nick wanted Angus to leave Dummie alone, but there was no way Angus was going downstairs. He stayed with Dummie even when he fell asleep again.

Angus' father left them on their own together but staggered back up the stairs every hour. After the third time, Dummie got up, wobbled over to Angus' desk and got the thickest felt tip pen he could find.

"Do you want to draw?" Angus asked. He was afraid that Dummie might have forgotten their language. But Dummie went over to his father, pulled up his trouser leg and wrote *DUMMIE* on his plaster in large letters. "MAASHI?" he whispered.

Angus and Nick looked at each other. Angus bit his lip which had begun to quiver again.

Nick gave him a tired smile. He stroked Dummie's head, stroked Angus' hair and then hobbled to the door. "I'm going to make pizza," he said. "We've got something to celebrate."

That evening the phone rang. Nick picked up. "Nick Gust... Oh, hello... Yes, everything's fine. It worked well. Dummie is awake— Yes, really. It's unbelievable. And you? ... How long? Yes, that's good. I really have to thank— Yes, alright. We'll talk tomorrow— Bye." He hung up. "That was Mr Scribble. He has to spend the night at the hospital. They didn't find anything, of course, but it's still necessary. He's coming over to see Dummie tomorrow. He said you'd done brilliantly."

"He did too," Angus said at once. "It wouldn't have worked without him. He was lying there groaning like a cow giving birth. You should have heard him."

His father burst out laughing. "How do you know what that sounds like? A cow giving birth?" he joked.

"It's just what I think. Or a pig." And then Angus had to laugh too, for the first time in ages.

CHAPTER 9

ALL Back To Normal

Well. Then everything got back to normal, as far as things could ever be normal with Dummie. The next morning Dummie felt much better, and in the afternoon, he sat downstairs again with Angus, watching television. Angus was allowed to spend the rest of the week at home with Nick. He called the school and said that both Dummie and Angus had flu. It gave them a chance to recover, they needed that, he said. His father had to recover too, Angus thought, because he just sat next to them in his red chair and didn't go to the shed once.

Mr Scribble was sent home in a taxi. At the end of

the afternoon, he cycled up their path as though he hadn't had a heart attack the day before. When he saw Dummie sitting on the sofa, he shook his head. "I never thought it would work," he said. "That alarm. It scared me so much I almost had a real heart attack."

"Apart from that, you look pretty healthy," Angus joked.

"So does Dummie," Mr Scribble said. "Well, erm, I mean—" He grinned as he looked at Dummie's brown face, "... for a mummy, he does."

Mr Scribble stayed for dinner and Nick made pizza again, now to celebrate the fact that Mr Scribble was better. But Angus thought he just felt like making pizza again, because Mr Scribble hadn't really been ill at all.

And that was that.

Within three days, Dummie was skipping around just as happily as before he got sick. He climbed the tree in the back garden again, played football, beat Angus at chess and played with his scarab in bed at night. He wouldn't be able to lose it again, because Nick had pinned the chain to his bandages with a safety pin.

On Sunday evening, they changed Dummie's bandages and on Monday, Dummie and Angus cycled to school together. Angus was a little nervous again. But on the way he decided that so much had happened over the last week that school would be easy. And before he got to school, he felt a bit better.

Mr Scribble was back at school again too. Everyone

was happy that he was back because they'd had a really annoying substitute teacher. All the children were happy that Angus and Dummie were back too. Dummie did stunts again, played football better than all the others and knew everything about Egypt. It was as though nothing had ever happened.

To Angus' total surprise, Miss Frick came to the door after the break. Her eyes behind the jam jar glasses were green again and she was as miserable as ever. But Angus saw a few brown spots on her face and red lines on her neck where the skin had torn when he'd grabbed her by the throat. She probably couldn't remember any of it, because when Angus hung back to look at her, she snapped at him that he was to hurry along.

She wasn't nasty to Dummie either. She must have forgotten everything, because otherwise she would have been frightened of the burned boy with that frightening scarab. Angus was convinced that it had almost killed her. It might have been better for all of them if Miss Frick had been frightened of Dummie. But when Angus told his father everything later, he thought it better this way.

Miss Paula saw Angus walking past and asked if he'd found his gym shorts and Angus simply said yes.

In front of the class Mr Scribble asked whether the police had found the scarab and Angus simply said yes.

And no one had recognised the scarab in the paper.

Angus had been worried about that, but even that hadn't happened. All the children had seen it, because clever Mr Scribble had brought the newspaper clipping along to school and hung it next to a poster of a pyramid. But nobody thought that Dummie's scarab and this one were one and the same. So they didn't spot that and Angus thought that was unbelievable too: Mr Scribble said that there was as strange scarab in the paper, so everyone saw a strange scarab. You see what you think you see.

Annalisa and Lizzy kept a low profile. They didn't know that the scarab was so powerful, and that Dummie had almost died. But they did know that Angus knew that Annalisa had taken Dummie's scarab and that was enough to keep them quiet.

In fact everything was just fine.

The schools' competition was two weeks later.

They travelled by bus to a large sports hall in the province's capital. Five classes from five other schools were there too. Dummie had never been in such a big camel on wheels and he loved it. He insisted on sitting up front and because he was the leader of the Hobble's team, Mr Scribble let him.

Angus sat on the chair behind him. Of course he was nervous again. No one gave Dummie a second glance in Polderdam anymore. But now all kinds of new people would see him. Nick had said that Angus should think about that day at the beach, but that didn't help much. By the time they were there, his stomach was sore.

They swarmed into the hall. Everyone screaming and shouting and Angus all quiet and anxious. In the middle of the room were six tables with three chairs at each table. There was a real public gallery all around them and a real jury. Dummie had a name badge pinned to him and proudly sat down in the middle seat at the Hobble table. After a while it grew silent. Angus saw him sitting there with his flap and cap and began to feel hot.

A lady with a microphone began to explain the rules of the competition. After that she walked over to the tables to introduce everyone. She slowly got closer to Dummie and Angus got hotter and hotter.

"Girls and boys, here we have Emma, Dummie and Ebbi from Hobble Primary," the lady cried. His class began to cheer all around Angus. It quietened down again and the lady was already moving on to the next table when someone from the audience suddenly shouted, "He's dressed up as a mummy!"

Angus' heart fluttered. A mummy!

But then Ebbi stood up. "You're wrong!" he cried out. "Dummie *is* a mummy! We had him flown in especially for the competition! Because we want to win!" Everyone had a good laugh about that.

Dummie stood up, walked over the lady, grabbed the microphone and said, "I am not a mummy. I am burned. But it doesn't ghurt. We are going to win the competition!"

And then the room exploded into cheers. Not because Dummie had said that his school was going to win, every school wanted to win, but because they found it so wonderful, that a boy with burns would dare to join in the competition. Because, believe it or not, from that moment onwards everyone in the hall saw exactly what Polderdam had seen for weeks: a burned boy with a cap on.

Then the competition began.

There were two hundred questions. There were easy questions and difficult ones. Dummie only gave the correct answer when none of the others knew it. Angus thought that was clever of him. And he felt so terribly proud that he got all hot again. But without a stomach ache.

The competition lasted three hours. One team was out, then another. In the end there were just two schools left. Now the room became quiet. But it wasn't that exciting. It was clear: the Hobbles knew everything. No, Dummie knew everything. And the Hobbles won easily. Because of Dummie.

After the last question, the entire room burst into

cheers. Dummie stood up and bowed. All the children were given a banner and the school was given a trophy, which Dummie, as their leader, raised in the air.

They all congratulated each other and before they knew it, they were back in the bus.

Angus was incredibly relieved. He sat next to Dummie, who was holding the trophy proudly on his lap. From time to time, he looked at him. He couldn't see Dummie's face, so he had to guess what Dummie was thinking. But he was probably grinning from ear to ear. Angus knew what that looked like and it was for the best that no one could see it.

He chuckled to himself. Dummie had spent the whole day not being a mummy. And then, at that moment in the bus, Angus began to believe in it himself: maybe Dummie would never have to be one again...

When they arrived in Polderdam, the rest of the school were waiting for them in the playground. Mr Scribble had telephoned ahead, of course. He was as proud as a monkey with a peacock tail.

Miss Frick was there too. As headmistress of the school, she would be presented with the trophy.

As soon as the door to the bus swung open, they all began to whoop and clap. Dummie got out first, held the trophy up high and they all made as much noise as they could.

Of course Miss Frick had to congratulate Dummie. She couldn't avoid it. Her face screwed up, she shook his hand. "Congratulations," she said curtly.

"You can say that again!" Mr Scribble cried. "We couldn't have done it without Dummie!"

Angus was standing right next to Miss Frick and heard her mutter, "At least he's good for something."

Mr Scribble heard it too. His eyes began to shine. "Dummie, give the trophy to Miss Frick," he said gently. Then he whispered something in Ebbi's ear.

Dummie didn't hesitate and held out the trophy to Miss Frick. Right at that moment, Ebbi began to

KISS!! KISS!! KISS

shout: "Kiss! Kiss!" They all giggled and then the whole playground was shouting out along with him: "Kiss! Kiss! Kiss!"

Dummie and Miss Frick looked at each other and Angus held his breath.

Dummie held up his hand to get their attention and it grew silent. Then all of a sudden, at the top of his voice, he shouted, "NO!"

Then they all laughed even more and Angus almost wet his pants, Miss Frick was pulling such a crazy face. She was laughing along, it was the only thing she could do, but like a farmer's wife with a toothache in all her teeth.

That evening, Angus, Dummie, Nick and Mr Scribble sat at the dinner table. They were having pizza with broccoli again, because they had something to celebrate. Mr Scribble had eaten with them four times over the past week and was just as used to Dummie's face as Angus and his father by now.

While the other three ate, Dummie kept on talking about the competition. Mr Scribble burst out laughing from time to time, and when Dummie told him indignantly that he'd never kiss Miss Frick in his whole life and said, "I will never kiss ugly face of that wuss!" Mr Scribble choked on his pizza three times in a row.

"What about if you win the national finals next month?" Nick joked.

Dummie pulled such a face that all three of them almost got scared. "No!" he said. Then he sat down in his chair and raised his arms in the air. "I am ghood!" he said proudly.

Angus looked at his ugly face and his shining eyes and completely agreed.

"Yes, you are very good," he said. And he hoped that Dummie would stay with them for the rest of his life. And how were they going to deal with that—? Well, his father would probably know.

ANOTHER BOOK ABOUT DUMMIE THE MUMMY!

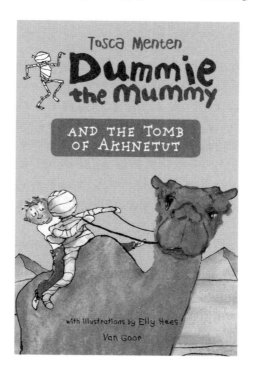

Dummie couldn't be happier. After an eventful journey he is finally back in Egypt to search for the grave of his father, pharaoh Akhnetut. Along with Angus and Nick, he sets out in good spirits. But after four thousand years, Egypt has changed entirely and Akhnetut's grave is nowhere to be found. Then something terrible happens and suddenly Angus and Dummy are in great danger...

DARWISHI UR-ATUM MSAMAKI MINKABH ISHAQ EBONI
RODE UP THE HILL ON HIS DONKEY AKILA. WHEN HE
REACHED THE TOP, HE GAZED OUT ACROSS THE DESERT.
KING SADIHOTEP THE GREAT, HIS FATHER'S FATHER,
WAS DEAD. THERE IN THE DISTANCE, HIS
GRANDFATHER'S PYRAMID WAS READY AND WAITING. IT
HAD ONLY JUST BEEN COMPLETED. LAST TIME THE NILE
FLOODED, THE BUILDERS HAD TAKEN THE FINAL STONES
TO THE TOP.

DARWISHI HAD EXPECTED HIS GRANDFATHER TO LIVE
FOR MANY MORE YEARS. BUT INSTEAD ALL OF A SUDDEN
HE'D DIED IN THE MIDDLE OF THE NIGHT.

DARWISHI TURNED AROUND SADLY AND LOOKED AT
THE MIGHTY BLUE-GREEN RIVER NILE. THE FLOODS HAD
ENDED OVER TWO MONTHS AGO AND THE LAND WAS
LUSH AND FERTILE. THEY HAD SADIHOTEP TO THANK FOR
THAT. SADIHOTEP HAD BEEN A GOOD KING. AND A VERY
KIND GRANDFATHER...

EGYPT BELONGED TO DARWISHI'S FATHER AKHNETUT
NOW. HIS FATHER WOULD HAVE TO TAKE CARE OF IT AS
WELL AS SADIHOTEP HAD. AND LATER, WHEN AKHNETUT
WAS GONE, DARWISHI HIMSELF WOULD BE KING AND
THIS FERTILE COUNTRY WOULD BE HIS...

FOR A MOMENT, DARWISHI FELT VERY PROUD. BUT

THEN HE PICTURED HIS GRANDFATHER'S SEVERE BUT
KIND FACE AGAIN. AND IMMEDIATELY AFTER THAT HE
THOUGHT OF THE TERRIBLE ROOM IN WHICH THEY HAD
TURNED HIS GRANDAD INTO A MUMMY. HE SHIVERED. IT
HAD TAKEN SEVENTY DAYS. HIGH PRIEST HEPSETSUT
HAD TAKEN HIM THERE A FEW TIMES. EACH TIME,
HEPSETSUT HAD EXPLAINED WHAT WAS HAPPENING. IT
HAD BEEN A TERRIBLE SHOCK FOR DARWISHI EACH TIME.
THE FIRST TIME, THERE WERE FOUR LARGE JARS NEXT
TO HIS GRANDFATHER'S BODY.

"WHAT PRETTY VASES. WILL THEY BE BURIED WITH
HIM TOO?" DARWISHI HAD ASKED CURIOUSLY.

"THEY ARE FOR HIS BRAINS AND ENTRAILS,"
HEPSETSUT HAD SAID.

"WHAT?!"

DARWISHI HAD RUN AWAY SCREAMING, AND HE HAD
SPENT THE WHOLE DAY THINKING ABOUT THEM TAKING
OUT HIS GRANDAD'S INSIDES AND PUTTING THEM IN THE
VASES.

THE SECOND TIME HE HAD TO GO ALONG, THEY WERE
SPRINKLING WHITE STUFF ALL OVER HIS GRANDAD TO
DRY HIM OUT. AND THE THIRD TIME THEY WERE
SPRAYING ALL KINDS OF OIL ON HIM.

"WHY DO I NEED TO KNOW ALL OF THIS?" DARWISHI
CRIED. "IT'S DREADFUL!"

BECAUSE YOU ARE THE PHARAOH'S OLDEST SON,"
HEPSETSUT SAID. "IT MEANS YOU'LL BE KING YOURSELF
ONE DAY. FROM NOW ON, YOU ARE NOT JUST TO LEARN
THE SECRETS OF LIFE BUT THOSE OF DEATH AS WELL.
WE ARE PREPARING YOUR GRANDFATHER'S BODY FOR HIS
JOURNEY. IF YOUR GRANDFATHER'S BODY IS PRESERVED,

HE CAN TRAVEL ON UNDISTURBED AND LIVE WITH THE
GOD OSIRIS FOR ALL ETERNITY."

AND SO HIS GRANDFATHER WAS TRANSFORMED FROM A
HANDSOME MAN INTO A WRINKLED MUMMY. AND TODAY
HE WOULD BE BURIED.

DARWISHI GUIDED AKILA TO THE TEMPLE BESIDE THE
NILE. THERE THE PROGRESSION BEGAN TO MAKE ITS
WAY ALONG THE LONG ROAD TO THE PYRAMID.

DARWISHI WAS ALLOWED TO RIDE AKILA IN THE
PROCESSION, BECAUSE HE HAD BEEN A GIFT FROM HIS
GRANDFATHER. IT MEANT HE HAD A GOOD VIEW.
HEPSETSUT WAS RIGHT AT THE FRONT. THEN CAME THE
OXEN THAT PULLED UP THE BOAT CONTAINING
SADIHOTEP, USING ROLLING TREE TRUNKS. BEHIND THEM
WALKED THE PRIESTS AND PRIESTESSES BEARING
OFFERINGS AND AFTER THEM, HIS FATHER AND MOTHER.
AT THE BACK WERE THE PEOPLE WHO LIVED IN THE
PALACE WITH THEM, AND THEN OTHER PEOPLE. THE
PROCESSION WAS NEARLY AS LONG AS THE ENTIRE ROAD.

DARWISHI GLANCED TO THE SIDE. HIS FATHER LOOKED
GOOD. AKHNETUT WAS WEARING THE DOUBLE CROWN OF
EGYPT, THE WHITE CROWN OF THE SOUTH AND THE RED
CROWN OF THE NORTH. IN THE MIDDLE OF THE CROWN,
THE POWERFUL GOLDEN SCARAB OF MUKATAGARA
GLITTERED. AND IN HIS HANDS, AKHNETUT CARRIED A
BRAND NEW GOLDEN SCEPTRE. WOULD DARWISHI LOOK
LIKE THAT HIMSELF ONE DAY? IT HARDLY SEEMED
POSSIBLE.

THEY SLOWLY WALKED ON. IT WAS HALF AN HOUR
BEFORE THE PROCESSION REACHED THE TEMPLE NEXT TO

Sadihotep's pyramid. The sound of people wailing in grief grew louder.

The bearers carefully lifted Sadhotep's body from the boat and disappeared into the pyramid with it.

Darwishi was allowed to go with them into the large square burial chamber.

He saw everything. Sadihotep in his stone sarcophagus. The scary jars. And all the treasures his grandad was taking with him, almost two rooms full. Even his grandad's golden chair was going on his journey with him.

Darwishi looked at the wall behind the sarcophagus. He'd done a picture for his grandfather on it. He had spent two whole days in the burial chamber painting three elegant birds with long necks. They were flying above the Nile during the floods. It was the nicest painting in the entire grave, he thought proudly.

It was almost over. As they chanted, the priests moved the heavy lid onto the sarcophagus. Finally, Hepsetsut placed Sadihotep's golden sceptre respectfully on his sarcophagus.

Then they walked backwards, bent over, through the pyramid's corridors until they were outside. Hepsetsut came last, smoothing over the sand with his feet as he went.

Offerings were still being set down in grandad's temple. People sang and danced. It almost seemed like a party, Darwishi thought angrily.

As the sun set, Hepsetsut sealed the grave and they finally went home.

Darwishi cried the whole night. His grandad had only just set off on his journey, but he missed him already...

Early the next morning, Hepsetsut came into his bedroom.

"Come with me," he whispered.

Darwishi got up and followed the high priest outside. A carrier chair with six bearers stood waiting for him in the dark.

"Where are we going?" Darwishi asked.

"Out."

"Out? To the village? Why?"

Hepsetsut put his hand on Darwishi's head. "One day the crown of Egypt will rest on your head," he said. "You will be king, Darwishi. That's why I want to show you how your people live, work and eat. From now on, I'll take you to the village every full moon. You must take good care of the people when you are older. You will lead their army, you will administer their justice, you will ensure peace, prosperity and eternal life. Whether the people do well depends on you. This is why you need to get to know them."

"But they're ordinary people. Won't dad mind?" Darwishi asked.

"I did the same with him," Hepsetsut said.

The bearers carried little Darwishi to the village. While the sun was born on the other

SIDE OF THE NILE, THEY ENTERED A HOUSE. PEOPLE
WERE EATING BEANS AND DRINKING BEER. WHEN THEY
SAW HEPSETSUT, THEY STOPPED EATING AND BOWED. A
DARK WOMAN WITH BLACK EYES FETCHED A PLATE WITH
THREE FISHES ON IT.

HEPSETSUT GAVE DARWISHI A FISH. IT WAS DRY AND
TASTED OF SALT.

DARWISHI ATE MORE FISH AND AFTER THAT HE HAD
BEANS. A STRANGE WOMAN PLACED A FLORAL GARLAND
BEFORE HIM ON THE FLOOR, AND A POT OF SCENTED OIL.
DARWISHI NODDED AWKWARDLY AND PICKED IT UP.

AFTER AN HOUR, THEY RETURNED TO THE PALACE.

"FROM NOW ON YOU WILL LEARN TO READ AND
WRITE. I WILL TEACH YOU TO FIGHT IN WARS, TO SWIM,
WRESTLE AND HUNT WILD ANIMALS. I WILL TEACH YOU
ABOUT RELIGION," HEPSETSUT SAID.

"BUT I CAN'T DO ANY OF THAT," DARWISHI SAID IN
CONFUSION.

HEPSETSUT SMILED. "I WILL HELP YOU," HE SAID.
"FROM NOW ON, EVERYTHING IS GOING TO BE
DIFFERENT—"

DARWISHI JOLTED AWAKE. HE OPENED HIS EYES, SAT UP
AND LOOKED AROUND. HIS NEW FRIEND ANGUS WAS
ASLEEP NEXT TO HIM. HIS NEW DAD, NICK, WAS LYING
IN THE OTHER BEDROOM. HIS HAND FELT FOR THE
CHAIN WITH THE SCARAB AROUND HIS NECK. IT WAS

THE SCARAB OF MUKATAGARA FROM HIS FATHER'S CROWN, AND THE ONLY MEMENTO OF HIS FATHER AND MOTHER HE HAD LEFT.

YET AGAIN HE HAD DREAMED OF THE PAST. AND AGAIN HE'D ALMOST FORGOTTEN EVERYTHING. IT HAD BEEN SOMETHING ABOUT A FUNERAL PROCESSION, AND HEPSETSUT. FOR THE PAST FEW DAYS, HE'D DREAMED EVERY NIGHT. DREAMS ABOUT HIS DONKEY, HIS FATHER, THE PEOPLE IN EGYPT. BUT WHEN HE WOKE UP, EVERYTHING WAS GONE. HE WAS NEVER BACK HOME. HE WOULD NEVER EAT SALTED FISH WITH HEPSETSUT AGAIN. HE WOULD NEVER BE PHARAOH AND HAVE HIS OWN PYRAMID. IT WAS FOUR THOUSAND YEARS LATER AND HE WAS IN A FOREIGN COUNTRY CALLED HOLLAND. EVEN HIS NAME WAS DIFFERENT. HE WASN'T CALLED DARWISHI ANYMORE BUT DUMMIE.

HE SLID OUT OF BED, WENT TO THE MIRROR IN THE BATHROOM AND LOOKED AT HIS DRIED-OUT FACE WITH ITS TORN LIPS AND GOLDEN EYES. HE CLOSED HIS EYES. NOW HE SAW HIS BLACK BRAIDED HAIR, FLAWLESS PALE BROWN SKIN AND PEARLY WHITE TEETH. WHEN HE OPENED HIS EYES AGAIN, HE LOOKED STRAIGHT INTO THE HOLE WHERE HIS NOSE HAD ONCE BEEN.

AFTER A WHILE HE TURNED AROUND AND WENT BACK INTO THE BEDROOM. HE CREPT QUIETLY BACK INTO BED AND CLUTCHED HIS SCARAB TIGHTLY IN HIS HAND.

DAD, HE THOUGHT. DAD, MUM. HE COULDN'T GET BACK TO SLEEP.